JABEZ

A NOVEL

THOM LEMMONS

WaterBrook
PRESS

JABEZ
PUBLISHED BY WATERBROOK PRESS
2375 Telstar Drive, Suite 160
Colorado Springs, Colorado 80920
A division of Random House, Inc.

Scripture taken from the *New King James Version.* Copyright © 1982 by
Thomas Nelson, Inc. Used by permission. All rights reserved.

ISBN 1-57856-563-4

Printed in the United States of America
2001—First Edition

10 9 8 7 6 5 4 3 2 1

Dedicated to the Laity Lodge
Artists' and Writers' Retreat,
July 2001

◤ ◥

In the days of the Judges, the people of Israel forgot their God and did evil in the eyes of the Lord. Israel had no king; every man did as he saw fit. And so the Lord gave Eglon, king of Moab, power over Israel for eighteen years. Again the Israelites cried out to the Lord, and he gave them a deliverer —Ehud, a left-handed man, the son of Gera the Benjamite.

*Now Jabez was more honorable
than his brothers...*

…and his mother called his name
Jabez,
saying, "Because I bore him
in pain."

And Jabez called on the God of Israel, saying,
"Oh, that you would bless me indeed,
and enlarge my territory,
that Your hand would be with me,
and that You would keep me from evil,
that I may not cause pain!"

So God granted him what he requested.

THE NAME

The first thing I remember was my mother's crying. Sometimes I think she fed me on her tears instead of her breast milk. Even then, long before she told me the story of my beginning, I think I tried to guess it in her eyes. A child sees many things that he cannot name.

And then, when I was old enough, I heard it in the taunts of the other boys in the village. "Hey, Pain-boy, it hurts me just to look at you." I was small for my age and an easy target for bullies. They tripped me and hit me and rolled me in the dirt. They told me they were making me match my name. They said it with a dirty laugh and an upturned lip. My brothers, especially, used my name that way. Like a switch on my backside or a lump of dung tossed at my feet.

I liked it when the Amalekites came through. They squatted on their mats in the square by the well with their camels tethered behind them. On the ground they spread their trinkets, their packets of spices, their god-totems and the shiny cloth woven with strange designs. I loved wandering among them, listening to the unfamiliar lilt of their words. When I said my name to the Amalekites, it was just a name. On their foreign tongues, "Jabez" meant me—nothing more. Jabez was the boy who talked to them, who wanted to know the names for things in their own language. He was not the boy with no father, the one who fit nowhere.

I was always sad when the Amalekites left. I longed to follow them, my longing as dry and hovering as the dust kicked up by their camels. I wanted to be away from the taunts, the mocking looks. Away from the despite of my brothers. And away from my mother's silent, dark weeping.

How does a boy know when he is the cause of pain? How can he give words to himself that he doesn't have? How can he understand why his presence is a wrongness, a hurt? I don't know. But so often when I heard my name in the mouth of someone who knew me, the wrongness slapped at me. My name was better to me when it came from the lips of strangers.

There was an old woman, Gedilah, who lived in our village. She wandered about Beth-Zur, talking as if someone was with her, but most always there was no one there. She would sit down beside my mother when she was grinding grain. She would talk to her. No one else in Beth-Zur would sit down and talk to my mother.

Sometimes I would see Gedilah on her way to the well, walking past our plot of scraggly olive trees. Sometimes, when I was pulling weeds from our chickpea patch beside the road, she would stop and settle her old, dry haunch atop the stone wall with a grunt. The bent woman would start talking to me. I don't know why.

Gedilah would talk like someone continuing a conversation she had started some other time. She had a few teeth left in the back of her mouth, but none in front. Her leathery lips flapped around the words and made it hard for me to understand her. As she spoke, she stared off at the horizon, at the straw-colored hills, creased with faint green, that surrounded Beth-Zur. Gedilah told me stories, but she never looked at me.

I knew of no one in the village older than this woman. She talked about the days of her mother, when our people had wandered through the desert, a time before we came to live in the

country between the Salt Sea and the Great Sea. A god had followed our people through the desert, she said, or maybe she said
the god led them. Why this god took such an interest, she did not
explain. She never even said the god's name. Once, when I asked
her, she said the god had no name. Or maybe her mother had told
her, but she had forgotten it. At night it was a fire god, and by day
it was a dust god, a towering whirlwind, she claimed.

"What good is a god with no name?" I asked her one time.
"How can you talk to it? How can you ask it for things?" Every-
body in the village had a few gods they kept in a safe, dark corner
of the house. They were of wood or clay or stone. People rubbed
them with oil and whispered in their ears and decorated them with
feathers or bits of cloth or daubs of paint. My oldest brother had
one that he carried out to the olive trees just before the winter rains
each year; it was a sitting woman with heavy breasts. To me it
looked like a small, fat water cup, but he said it was the Great Lady
of Moab and that her womb was the earth. He kept the basin in
her lap full of oil, and sometimes he mixed in the blood of a pigeon
or a rock badger. He said she would protect our olive trees and
make them bear. From the look of our trees most years, I sometimes wondered why he didn't try a different god.

But the desert god, the woman said, had no name and no
image. "What would a desert god need with an image?" she said.

"He blows with the wind; he shimmers in the heat. He is. That's all I can say."

Maybe that was why for so long I never heard anyone but the old woman talk about this god. What did we need with a desert god? We weren't wanderers anymore. We had settled down. We had groves and vineyards and fields. We had flocks. We needed gods for seed and bearing, not for roaming.

Still, something in me ached for roaming. At night in the summers, when the heat drove us to the housetop, to peel off all but the most needful clothing and lie limp as rags hoping for a breeze, I lay on my back and stared up at the stars. They hovered close, glittered like tears in the eyes of a hurt child. I tried to imagine their names, tried to call out to them. I wanted to know what they knew, look on all the lands they could see. I lay still and listened. Sometimes, I thought I could hear—something. Maybe it was the heat singing in my head. It could have been no more than the shrilling of my own blood. But it could have been something else.

My mother was neither ugly nor beautiful, though I suppose she had once been pleasing enough to look at. She was of normal size, but in my memory she is always small. Even as a child, I felt a need to be careful with her, the way you have to be careful with babies or sick people. Since I was the youngest in the household, I was the one at her beck and call. I was her errand runner, her helper. I fetched and held and stirred and carried for her. As best I can bring to mind, she struck me but a single time in all my life, and I guess I deserved that one blow. She almost never spoke harshly to me. But neither do I remember her smiling at me or singing to me. I think I would have endured a beating every day if it would have bought me her smile.

Gedilah's tiny little hut was not far from our house. Sometimes she would come and help my mother with the spinning or the churning. Sometimes my mother would send me to her with a little bit of meal or some oil in a small pouch. Gedilah and my mother would speak of times before I was born. Once I heard Gedilah telling my mother, "If he had lived, this child would not." My mother motioned at me with her eyes, and Gedilah said no more. She patted my head when she left.

My brothers paid my mother no mind. As long as there was something in the stew pot and their sandal straps got mended, they kept to themselves. I think they would have forgotten her if they could. But she was there, a constant reminder. And as if that weren't enough, I was there too. Mostly, they looked away.

I noticed, even as a child, that when I went with her to the well, the other women kept their faces turned from her. Their talk melted away when we came near, then resumed again as we passed. The other women would help each other settle their pitchers and urns on their heads. My mother had only me.

Sometimes I wanted to ignore her too. Sometimes the silence that surrounded her made me feel ashamed or sad or wrong. But now I know why I could not treat her as the others did; it was because she, at least, saw me. Even if she looked at me with eyes full of tears, my mother would not turn away her face the way everyone else did. Even if the most accustomed language between the two of us was silence, that was better than scorn. A sparse diet for one so hungry, but better than nothing.

Often, in the evening, she would go alone into the hills. A few times I followed, at a distance. When the sun was touching the rim of the world, she would walk out in the orange light, down the road until she turned aside at the draw that led to the pastures of Tubal and his sons. She would follow the ravine's crooked climb into the hills, picking her way among the rocks. Now and then, she would have to stop and free her garments from the grasp of a thorn bush or the spines of the briars that clung to the dry cracks between the boulders. She would climb until she came out on the breast of the Hill of Zur. She would go to the top and stare toward the west.

For a long time she would stand there, as still and straight as a pole, until the sun had dropped below the edge of the earth and the purpling night began to drift across from the east. I saw her lips move, though I was never close enough to hear any sound. Sometimes, I think, her eyes would be closed. And then, after a while, whatever secret thing pulled her there told her the time was long enough, and she turned to go the same way she had come. I would scamper out of sight to reach home before her.

I don't think anyone but me ever saw my mother perform her lonely, silent ritual. Most likely, no one else cared enough to notice. When she came back, I tried to read her face when she wasn't looking. I tried to see if her time on the hilltop had made any difference. But I could never see any change in her.

I had a certain dream of my mother that came to me several times as a boy. In my dream, I am walking through the doorway of our house. I am carrying something—a jar of oil, a sack of flour, I don't know—and I'm bringing it to her. When I come in, my mother is sitting on her mat, and black things are flying all around her head. At first I think they are birds, but when I look closer I see that they have many legs and jointed bodies, like insects. Their flying makes a clicking noise, like dry bones rattling together. I try to cry out, but no sound will come from my mouth.

She is looking at me and holding out her arms, but I cannot go to her because I know that she will clasp me to her and the black things will have me, too. I drop whatever it is I carried into the house and run outside, but instead of the street of our town I am running up a mountain of sand, the kind I have since seen in the wastes of the Arabah. I had never known such a sight as a boy, but that is the way of dreams. I am running up the side of the sand mountain, but with each step the loose sand slides under my feet. I cannot make any headway. When I am tired from trying to run in the sand and my breath feels hot in my throat, I stop and turn around. There is my mother, standing at the base of the sand mountain, still holding out her arms to me. The black flying things are gone now, but I am afraid they will come back. I want to go to her but I am afraid. I sit down in the sand and weep.

Each time I woke from this dream, I felt a terrible sadness, like a heavy bundle tied to my chest. Sometimes, in the dark, I would hold my breath and listen for the clicking sound. If I had known the name of a god of dreams, I would have asked it to take this dream away and never let it come back. I would have given it oil and some choice bit of meat. But I didn't know the name of a god for dreaming.

CHAPTER TWO

THE BINDING

I think it was about my tenth summer when my oldest brother took a wife. She was the daughter of Rekem, the one-legged dung gatherer. It was not a good match for either of them, but probably the best they could do. What wedding price could my brother pay, with nothing but a small grove of olive trees, a barley field, a few struggling grapevines, and a chickpea patch? What dowry could Rekem send with his daughter? Rekem spent his days crutching about with a basket, filling it with the pills that fell from the sheep and goats of other men, the thick pies that fell from their cows. He spread the dung to dry in the sun, then sold or traded it for food. Maybe my brother hoped for free fuel for the rest of his days from his new father-in-law. Maybe Rekem thought a claim on our sad little grove was better than nothing.

Ahuzzah, Jashub's bride, was short and round, like my brother's Moabite god. I don't know how she got so plump on such food as her father could afford. Her cheeks were so thick I rarely saw her teeth, even when she smiled or ate. She ate much more often than she smiled.

There was no wedding feast, no eating and drinking and loud exchange of vows. My brother just handed Rekem his sandal, then brought his bride to our house. When my mother saw the two of them coming, she hurried me out of the house. The water jars were full, but she said we needed to go to the well. As we neared the house on the way back, she called out my brother's name. I thought that was odd and I looked at her, but she would not look at me. When we came in, my brother was sitting beside the firepit, feeding tinder to a bluish curl of smoke. Ahuzzah sat on my brother's mat, cleaning her fingernails with one of my mother's bronze knives.

"What is there to eat?" Ahuzzah said.

———

The moon waxed and waned nine times, and Ahuzzah gave my brother a son. She started talking about it before the end of that first summer, maybe two full moons after Jashub brought her to live with him. I was surprised; I hadn't noticed any swelling of her stomach as there usually is with women. But I guess the swelling was all on the inside of her. If she had swollen any more on the outside, she would have burst like a melon left too long in the sun.

Once Ahuzzah was sure of the child in her womb, she couldn't be troubled to do so much as get herself a cup of water from the urn. Jashub kept himself busy with the trees and crops—anything to be away from his wife's nattering and mewling. My other brothers, Ishma and Anani, built themselves a lean-to behind the house just so they wouldn't have to sleep in the same room with her. I was glad to be old enough to work in the field and the orchard. It was better to be badgered and harried by my brothers than nagged by Ahuzzah. But all the weight of her upkeep fell on my mother, and Ahuzzah used her like a pack animal.

All day long she plopped on her mat like a bag of wet sand. She'd send my mother for a moistened rag to lay on the back of her neck, or she'd whine for some bread dipped in oil. "Could you please, Mother Libnah…" "Oh, Mother Libnah, if I only had…" She helped herself to the latrine, but little else.

The baby came in the fall, just after the first rains. It was a sudden thing; there wasn't even time for my mother to send me to

Gedilah. I had to help with the birthing. Ahuzzah yowled like she was being skinned alive.

My mother took the tiny, bloody bundle from between Ahuzzah's slick thighs. She cinched the purplish, ropy cord with clean woolen thread and cut it with her best knife. She called my brother in from his pacing to the place where the boy child lay, on the flat birthing stone near the firepit. Jashub stared at his panting wife for a moment, then picked up his son. Holding the infant away from him like a knot of soiled rags, he said, "His name is Plenty." The rains were good that year and the olive harvest a little better than usual, so that was surely as good a name as any. When my brother pronounced the name, he suddenly made a disgusted face. Jashub shoveled his son into my mother's arms and half ran out the door, slinging the newborn's dark, oily offal from his hand. My mother began cleaning the child and rubbing him with salt.

Jashub had little Raboth cut on the eighth day, mostly to please my mother. We had to send to Hebron for the old man who knew the ritual. He said some words I couldn't make out, then made a quick motion with his blade. Raboth gave a yelp and the old man daubed charcoal on the wound. Ahuzzah offered the baby a breast and the noise of his sucking quickly filled the room. My mother gave the old man a flask of oil and some hard cheese and thanked him for coming. I think my brother took the tiny flap of skin and burned it for his god.

I watched him with some fascination, this skinned rat of a boy. I watched him wriggle and squawk as his bindings were changed. I watched as Raboth gained the first of the tiny freedoms that would one day loose him into manhood: rolling from his back to his belly, writhing across the floor like a newt, raising himself on all fours to wobble like a clumsy puppy.

He was as helpless as a blind kitten. He soiled himself and lay in it until my mother cleaned him or the stink got bad enough for Ahuzzah to do it herself. He vomited curdled milk down his chin. He had to be constantly guarded from tumbling into the firepit or toppling an urn onto himself. If he could reach a clod of dirt, he would as soon eat that as a piece of bread.

But for all his weakness, for all his bondage to everyone and everything in his small world, he owned something I would never have. When my brother picked him up from the birthing stone and pronounced his name, he gave Raboth a place and a future. This puling, odorous suckling would inherit from Jashub. My brother's name would live through him. He had the blessing of a father. He belonged.

I wondered about my father. Why did he allow my mother to give me a name worse than no name? Did he even know when I was born? No one ever talked about him to me, even my brothers. Especially my brothers. At least they were old enough when he died to remember something about him. But to me, my father was an emptiness, a nothing. The lack of him bound me, fixed the limits of what I might become. The absence of this man I would never know had set a fence about me, and there was nothing I could do to change it.

Raboth grew as fat and slick as a little grubworm. Ahuzzah coddled him and jounced him in her lap. He climbed on her like a big, soft pillow. He poked his fingers in her ears, her mouth. He gabbled baby talk into her face and drooled on her cheeks, and she laughed and played finger games with him. Watching her with her son brought me as near as I ever came to liking Ahuzzah.

When he was old enough to totter about on his bowed legs, he sometimes tried to follow me. He jabbered at me until I turned to look at him. He stretched out his arms to me.

"No, Raboth. You have to stay here."

He squalled and made fists. He started toward me and his hurry toppled him. He sat down hard in the dirt and squealed with infant fury. It made me laugh.

"Sorry, little wart. When you're older."

Ahuzzah ambled over and scooped him into the crook of an arm. She gave me a blaming look, then carried him back to whichever shaded corner she was roosting in. Raboth yelled and tried to climb out of her arms.

One evening just before supper I heard her telling Jashub to keep me away from the baby. "Raboth is your blood, not that half-brother," she said. "He has no business with our son." Jashub kept his eyes on whatever else he was doing, as he usually did when she talked to him. But I noticed him watching me differently after that.

———

The following spring, the Amalekites had a new thing when they unpacked their wares: the hard metal of the sea people. They had knives, pruning hooks, even a few sickles. Iron they called it, and it was harder than even the best bronze. My brother and all the men in Beth-Zur coveted it. But it was very dear; even old Tubal could afford only a few sickles and some shearing blades for his sons' herdmen. Only the sea people knew the secret of its forging, the Amalekites said, and they guarded the knowledge closer than they guarded their wives. The Amalekites said the streets of the sea people's cities jangled with the stuff. On the broad roads running along the coast of the Great Sea, the princes of the sea people rode in chariots with iron-rimmed wheels. I could not imagine such wealth.

That spring, the spring of iron, was when the cattle raids

started to the east of us. Some of the men in the square started to talk about herds lost in the night, of herdsmen gutted and left to the carrion birds and the jackals in the hills. We began to see the smudge of distant burnings and smell the smoke on the wind from the eastern deserts. Stragglers from the clans on the other side of the Salt Sea came through, some with wounds hastily bound, some carrying the dead and dying. Their eyes were like those of a deer caught in a snare. Eglon of Moab had risen against them, they said. He swarmed across the Arnon River with his Ammonite and Amalekite mercenaries and sacked Aroer, Dibon, and Kiriathaim. He made their women watch as he killed their men, then he gave the women to his soldiers.

"He will come here," they said. "His eye looks next upon these green lands across the Jordan."

My brothers Ishma and Anani were hot for the fight. "We should arm ourselves," Anani said. He was as thin and spare as a wild goat, but the muscles of his arms were stringy and tough, like knots in a rawhide thong. His beard had just started to grow in downy tufts along the lower line of his jaw. "Our people took this land once. We can take it again."

Ishma said the same. Surely people in other villages were gathering to make plans, he said, and so must we. The men of Judah should not be afraid to face Eglon. Were we nothing, that the king of Moab should tread on us without fear? Were the clans of Reuben and Gad not our kin, that strangers should be allowed to despoil them? In their lean-to at night I heard them talking in low, tight voices. I heard them telling each other the old stories of Father Caleb and the taking of Hebron and Debir, of Othniel and his overthrow of Cushan the Doubly Wicked.

But Jashub looked at his wife and his little boy, sleeping in the corner, and would not join in his younger brothers' war talk. Beth-Zur was a small place, he said. We had nothing of interest to Eglon. Why should we care what happens in Gad or Reuben, or even in the City of Palms? He had trees here to tend and crops to gather in his fields. He did not have time to go somewhere else and fight over the troubles of other folk.

"I do not know why the songs of battle sing so loud in the blood of young men," my mother said to Gedilah one day.

Jashub had made me come to the house to scoop ash out of the firepit for scattering on the chickpea patch. The two women were leaned against the wall just outside one of the windows, picking gravel and chaff from a large bowl of barley. It was one of the times when Gedilah's mind was not wandering in unknown places. I gathered the ash with my hands and listened.

"Sometimes I wonder how there can be anyone left for killing."

"There has always been killing," Gedilah said. "There will always be killing."

I scooped the ash into the basket, and I watched as the fine dust rose up to drift on the air. It would settle after a while; it would leave a faint, gray trace on the water jars in the corner, on the wooden ladle my mother used to stir the stew pot. We would drink it, we would eat it. It would sift into the pile of wool my mother was gradually turning into thread. We would wear it in our clothing. I would put it on the chickpea patch, and it would become part of the plants, part of our food. The leftovers from the burning would become a part of us, a part of our surroundings, like the soot on the rough beams holding up the low roof.

"It is the men," Gedilah said. "The young ones learn it from the old ones."

"They should teach them other things," my mother said. "Surely there are other things."

My basket was nearly full. Still I sat beside the firepit, listening to the voices of my mother and Gedilah, letting the sound of their words sift into me like settling ash. I tried to imagine myself as a soldier. I thought of what it would be like to march north with Ishma and Anani and the other men, to camp in the open country. I wondered what stories fighting men told each other. I wondered if they sang songs to brace up their courage.

"They teach things even when they aren't trying," Gedilah said. "They can't help it."

"As my husband taught me the bitterness of mistrust?"

"Now, Libnah. Do you want to open that wound again?"

"What is the difference? The hurt of it never leaves me."

"And you have passed it on to your son."

My mother said no more after that.

If a man did well in a battle, would anyone care about his name, his father? If he saved the lives of his fellows and fought bravely for his kin and clan, would his past make any difference? Maybe that was why Ishma and Anani were eager to go north. They wanted the chance to claim the rights of men who have done a hard thing and earned its reward. If I had been older and they would have allowed it, I might have gone with them.

They left with the warming of spring. With maybe twenty other men of our town, they went to muster at a valley just south of Gilgal. A host of something like a thousand men gathered from the clans of Judah and Benjamin to go up against Eglon, we later heard. They were armed with mattocks, shearing knives, whatever they could find. Some of the richer ones had swords of iron and wooden shields with bullhide stretched across them. Eglon had just taken the City of Palms, and their plan was to attack while he was still in a place without walls. I don't remember the name of the one who led them. Maybe there was a leader for each muster. The designs of too many generals would partly explain what happened.

For days and days we heard nothing. I noticed many women in Beth-Zur going about with tight lips and worried eyes. Anxious words were exchanged at the well; old men muttered and shook their heads.

Just before midsummer, a few travelers came through from the north. They brought the news everyone had dreaded but no one had spoken aloud: The host of Israel had suffered a shameful defeat.

Mothers and wives keened at the doorways of their houses. Fear and uncertainty hung in the air like smoke. Jashub shook his head and said nothing. My mother spent whole days staring at the center of our firepit.

Then, in the depths of the dog days, a few heat-shriveled men came slinking into Beth-Zur by night. Some of them were missing limbs. Some of them had festering wounds partly bound up with dirty, crusted rags. One man, a friend of Jashub, had a raw gouge where the left side of his face had been. All of them were broken on the inside.

Ishma and Anani were among them. Anani's right hand was a useless clump of half-healed flesh and mangled bone. Ishma's body was unharmed, but he moved like a child's string toy; his eyes were blank pits of despair.

Slowly the story came out. At its root was the betrayal of the host by someone sympathetic to the Moabites; likely one of the Hivite freeholders in Ephraim. There was an ambush one night as the army slept. Hundreds of men were gutted where they lay. Ishma and Anani got away, with a handful of others, only because they were on a scouting mission away from the camp. They skulked and hid like beasts while the Moabite regulars scoured the countryside for any remainder of the rebel army. By the time they reached home, they were nearly like wild beasts themselves.

Anani eventually learned to do with his left hand what his maimed right could no longer accomplish; Ishma saw and heard things on that disastrous campaign that woke him screaming for the rest of his life.

In the fall, when the rains started and all the harvests were completed, Eglon sent three squadrons of soldiers to Beth-Zur. They were there to collect tribute from those who had rebelled against the just rule of the great Eglon, they said. As we watched, they went from house to house, from storage barn to storage barn, and loaded the grain that we would have used to feed ourselves and plant our crops for the next year. They took the oil from our groves, the wine and raisins from our vines. They took the best of our flocks. One of our men protested at the amount and a soldier killed him in front of his wife and children.

Three or four of the village fathers went with the guarded wains to Jericho. There, in the City of Palms, they had to fall on their faces in front of the fat Moabite king and say praise words to him. They had to rub ashes on their heads and in their beards. They had to swear by their seed that the village of Beth-Zur would be loyal to the just rule of the Regent of the Great Lady. And they had to promise to do it all again the next year, and the next year, and the next.

CHAPTER THREE

THE SEARCHING

T he tribute to Eglon would cripple us all during the years I grew to manhood, and beyond. Jashub was right: He still had trees to tend and crops to raise. But now the best of the olives and the firstfruits of the field went into the larder of Eglon. He made himself even fatter on the hunger of the people he had beaten.

When I think of those years, I always think of my mother's face. I think of it because the oppression of Eglon did not alter it. Alone of all the people in Beth-Zur, my mother seemed unsurprised by the hard times. Where others muttered behind their hands and called down secret curses on all Moabites and especially their king, my mother seemed to take almost no notice of our harsh conditions. Maybe her heart was already so pillaged that the circumstances of our people made little difference to her. Her secret grief was already so heavy that the addition of a little hunger, a little fear was not enough to attract her notice.

Each day rose like the reminder of a hateful duty. For a long time, Jashub had only me to help him keep oil in the jars and mush in our pot after packing off the choicest yield to the Moabite agents.

My mother was left at home with a daughter-in-law, who carried on much as if nothing in her life had changed, and a whining boy-child. Not that I blame Raboth; his little belly had forgotten what it was to be full, as had every belly in Beth-Zur. And for a time, my mother cared for Ishma and Anani as well. I saw her take mush out of her own bowl to let Raboth have an extra portion. I saw her sit by Ishma's pallet, wiping his forehead and cheeks when the night terrors took him.

She made her solitary walks to the hilltop. She spoke to the silence in words no one else could hear. I watched her and I wondered.

I wondered how she could shoulder so much hurt and still have eyes to see the hurt in someone else. I wondered what story she told herself to keep going, to help her endure with such quietness when each day seemed longer than the one before. I wondered: What was the truth of her suffering? And I tried to decide if I really wanted to know.

―――――――

Gedilah came to our house sometimes in the heat of the day, when everyone else in the village was drowsing in the shade. She slipped sideways through the doorway, as if trying to pass beneath the entry flap without touching it. Sometimes she just sat by the fire-pit and sifted the cold ashes between her fingers. Sometimes she sat with her eyes closed, rocking herself back and forth to a song only she could hear. Sometimes she would start talking, and it was hard to tell if she was talking to my mother, to everyone within earshot, or just to herself.

"Father Trickster came to a river," she said one day, "and he sent his wives and children and slaves and herds across the river. He waited until it was night, then he lay down to sleep."

"What are you talking about?" Ahuzzah said. She was on her mat, trying to lie down and shell chickpeas at the same time. Raboth was splayed against the wall, asleep.

"But a man grabbed him from the dark," the old woman said,

"and Father Trickster fought with him. He fought, but he could not best him. They fought until it was almost morning, and when the stranger saw he could not throw Father Trickster, he touched his leg and threw it out of joint."

My mother was sitting in a corner, her eyes on Gedilah. She was tossing milk in a skin, making cheese. The sound was steady. It twined among the words of Gedilah's story, like the tapping of a drum while someone sings a song. I lay on the packed earth of the floor, resting from the morning's work, trying to soak in what little coolness remained in the ground before going back out into the heat. It was the third summer of the Moabite time.

"'Who are you?' the stranger asked Father Trickster, and he answered, 'Jacob,' for that is the sound of his name in our ancient tongue. 'No more is your name Jacob,' the stranger said, 'for you have wrestled with me and with your brothers, yet you have not perished.' Then the stranger was gone. And forever after, Father Trickster walked with a limp."

There was a long quiet.

"What was the stranger's name?" Ahuzzah said. "You forgot that part." My mother rolled her eyes.

But the old woman was asleep.

That night I had a tangled dream. I was running on the shores of the Salt Sea, trying to get away from a wall of flame that followed me, pushed by the wind. I tripped on a root, then realized it was not a root, but the hand of a Moabite soldier. I fought with him as the fire roared and crackled around us. He wrestled me to the ground, then sat on my chest and pinned my arms at my sides. He wanted to know my name, but I couldn't remember. He began to curse and hit me, but I still couldn't tell him my name. Finally, I was able to push him aside, and at once I saw my mother kneeling on the shore, rubbing water from the Salt Sea on her face. Then the Moabite and my mother were gone, and the flame had gathered together all in one place, rising up into the dark sky like a watch fire.

When I woke in the morning, the first thing I saw was my mother, leaning over a bowl, washing her face. For an instant I expected to feel the Moabite on my chest, to hear the snicker and bellow of the fire. But then I remembered my name and knew I was awake.

Everyone else was asleep. I went outside to relieve myself. When I turned back, my mother was kneeling at the side of the house, pouring grain into a mortar. She took up the pestle and began to grind.

I stood watching for a bit, then went over and sat cross-legged on the ground across from her. Her eyes flickered toward me, then back to her task.

I asked her what she knew of the desert god from the long-ago time.

The pestle slowed, then resumed. "It was not so long ago," she said.

"Why does no one remember it then?"

The pestle crunched against the chickpeas, the sides of the mortar. She said nothing.

I told her I thought I had dreamed of this god.

She dropped the pestle into the mortar and held her face with both hands. When she took up the pestle again, her eyes were red and damp.

"He has taken my love, and now he takes my son."

"Who?"

She shook her head.

"Will you not tell me?"

Her hands stilled and she looked at me. Suddenly I did not want to hear. If the thought of this god could bring such instant pain to one who had suffered as quietly as my mother, I thought her words might be better left unsaid. I started to get up.

"No. Stay."

"What is the god's name?"

"He has no name."

"Then he cannot be much of a god."

She slapped me. The movement of her hand was quick and unexpected, like an adder striking from beneath the edge of a boulder. I fell backward in surprise.

"You are a foolish boy. Do not speak of things when you know nothing about them."

I rubbed my cheek and stared at her. She went back to her grinding, twisting the pestle against the grain as if it were an enemy.

"It is a bad thing to speak so about a god," she said a moment later.

A thought raised up to look at me. "The stranger in the story the old woman told—was that the god?"

She nodded. "Gedilah is old and her wits are half scrambled, but she remembers the old stories."

"Why would a god want to wrestle with a man? If he can throw a man's leg out of joint with a touch of his hand, why would he take the time to wrestle?"

The pestle paused, then went on. "I don't know. That you will have to find out for yourself."

It would be many years before I would begin to understand what she had said, what she had left out, and why.

That night I waited until everyone was asleep, then got up off my mat and padded outside and up the stairs to the roof. I lay on my back and looked at the stars for a while, trying to pray to the desert god with no name. I could not think how to talk to a god I knew nothing about. I decided to roll onto my stomach and cover my head with my hands to show respect. I had heard gods like to know you're not hiding anything from them in your fist. With my face in the packed clay and mud of the roof, I started praying.

"I do not know why you came to me in a dream of fire," I said. "I don't even know for sure if it was you who came, or if my mind dragged up some old scrap of something half remembered. But if you came, please tell me who you are, that I may call on you."

I lay very still, listening. I had never heard a god speak, so I didn't know what I was listening for. A voice from the shadows, maybe, as in Gedilah's story. Or a voice inside my head, like thought. Some sound of power—thunder from a clear sky, or a noise like the crashing of the sea on rocks. The sound of wind.

But there was nothing. Only the night noise of crickets and, far off, the yipping of jackals in the ravines. Once I felt a slight breeze run up my back and I thought the god was about to speak. My mouth went dry and a tingle ran down the back of my neck. But it was only wind.

Maybe the god wanted me to challenge him, fight with him like Father Trickster. Maybe the desert god was like the Amalekite traders: You had to dicker with him and prod him with gentle insults to get a better offer from him.

"Are you stronger than the Lady of Moab? Maybe you are not. The Lady of Moab has taken your land and the people that used to be yours. Maybe she will grow fatter than Eglon on the offerings of our people, and you will get hungry, as we are hungry now. Maybe you will get even weaker. Maybe she will take everything away from you and you will be disgraced and starving and completely forgotten."

I stopped talking and bit my lip. Maybe I had said too much this time. Pretty harsh words to offer a god, even a god with no name. I think my own hunger was talking. I think I wanted someone to pay for Anani's hand, for Ishma's shriveled will. I think my mother's slap was still stinging my face, and I wanted an accounting.

I waited with my nose mashed into the roof. I listened to the crickets and the jackals. There was no breeze at all now, only complete stillness. I waited until my hands went numb from being laced together for too long on the back of my head.

I raised myself to my knees. My hands started to wake up; they felt like they were being bitten by midges.

"If you will not answer me, then do not send me any more dreams," I said.

I waited a while longer, then went back down into the house. Raboth had rolled away from his mother's side in his sleep. His foot was dangling over the edge of the firepit. I scooted him over onto the mat beside Ahuzzah. He gave a little sigh, smacked his lips, and threw his arm across her belly. He never opened his eyes. I went to my pallet and lay for a long time, staring up at the ceiling. After a while I slept. I had no dreams that night, or for many nights to come.

CHAPTER FOUR

THE MISSION

I was eighteen the summer Eglon sent his bullies to Beth-Zur to gather an assault force at the point of the sword. They forced us—along with men from Hebron and Tekoa—to go up against the men of Jebus. That citadel on a hill had been a pebble in Eglon's shoe from the time he sat his fat haunches down in Jericho. The place was easily defended, and for all his trying he was unable to root out the resistance there.

They marched us to Bethlehem. They threw a fence around us, like cattle, and pulled us out a few at a time to pound and curse into us the arts of battle. They scattered us out among the Amalekite and

Ammonite troops. They didn't trust us with weapons, so most of us were to be sappers. Our taskmasters promised us on the names of all their gods that if we slacked, they would kill both us and all whom we'd left behind in our villages and towns.

We marched on Jebus about a week later. The city sits high on a rocky hill. A valley runs beneath the walls; it is impossible to come upon the citadel from any side without being seen.

The task of the sappers was to climb up the ridge to the base of the walls and dig ourselves in. We had bullhides stretched on poles that were supposed to ward off the arrows of the defenders above us. Once we had come to the walls, we were supposed to use fire, mattocks, wedges, or anything we could to open a breach in the fortifications. We were supposed to do this while the Jebusites hurled stones on us from above. The sappers looked up the rocky slope at the walls, then we looked at each other. There were no crevices, no hidden angles we could find to ward off the defenders as we worked. Our lives were worth nearly nothing, and we knew it.

The next morning, just before sunrise, they formed the sappers into loose ranks and handed us our tools. We were hedged with spears as they marched us to the foot of the ridge. We stood there in the half-dark, waiting for the command to advance. Though it was far from cool, I felt myself shivering. I could hear the breathing of the man beside me; it sounded like the panting of a wounded animal.

The order came and we scrambled up the rocks like ground squirrels. I heard the arrows of the defenders purring through the air around my head and rattling on the ground all about me. We had moved maybe ten strides when the pole bearer beside me took a shaft in the eye. I grabbed his pole and we kept going.

Behind us, the Moabite infantry gave a great shout and rushed forward. Some of the shooting from the walls was redirected at them, which is likely why my group was able to reach the base of the wall. Even so, the arrows punched at the bullhide like hawks striking at prey. Some of them came partway through. I knew the bullhide could not hold forever.

We wedged the poles with stones and started to dig at the walls. There were no forests to speak of anywhere close to Jebus, so fire was not a tool we could use. We pounded wedges into any crack we could find and flailed at them with our mallets. We dug in the flinty soil with our mattocks.

The infantry was making slow progress up the slope, coming beneath a canopy of bullhide and wooden shields and trying at the same time to return enough of a barrage to make the defenders cautious. When one of the foot soldiers fell, the rest stepped over him, closed ranks, and kept coming. At the rear of the advancing line they were bringing ladders.

I was crouched against the base of the wall, trying to press myself into the stones, when I saw something spatter against the rocks at the edge of our bullhide shelter. It hissed and bubbled against the ground. It was hot pitch. I looked up and saw some Jebusites heaving a heavy cauldron onto the parapet above us.

I cried out to my fellows. I pointed up, then at the Moabite infantry. I dashed out from under the bullhide just as the deluge of steaming pitch came down. I heard screaming behind me. Arrows clattered against the rocks as the two or three of us remaining dodged back and forth, trying to reach the line of shields.

The man closest to me went down; an arrow was in his leg. I grabbed for him and half-carried him down the hill. My foot hit a loose piece of shale and we fell. We rolled and tumbled and somehow fetched up against the legs of the front ranks of the infantry.

The assault was thrown back; the Moabite commander gave the signal to fall back. The infantry backed down the slope, and my wounded comrade and I went with them. I pulled the shaft from him while he bit on a stick from a tamarisk. I cleaned and bandaged the wound as best I could. I heard later that the wound went bad and the man died from it.

When we had been encamped outside Jebus about a week, one of the commanders had me brought before him. He looked me up and down and nodded. He said something in the lazy, slurred Moabite tongue to one of his servants, and they took me to another place. When I got there, a wiry old desert man with a bald head told me I was going with him and two others on a special errand. "You're small enough to crawl into the place," he said. "But I'll have an arrow pointed at your back, just in case you try to get clever." He told me to come back just before nightfall.

The moon was overhead when night fell, and we had to wait until it had set. In the dark, we picked our way around the edge of the ravine below the walls of the city to a place on the eastern side of the base of the ridge. The old man hobbled me with ankle ropes to prevent me from escaping in the dark. The hill of the fortress rose up from the place where we crouched, and the walls rose higher still. I had to tilt my head back to see the stars.

"A water shaft is there somewhere," the old man whispered, pointing up the slope to a cleft between some large, flat stones. "If you scamper up there in a hurry, the Jebusites might not shoot you." He gave me a nasty grin while he was untying my ankle ropes. He told me I was supposed to find the opening and see if it went all the way into the city. I was supposed to come back and tell him. If I brought good news, I would be rewarded. "Unless," he said, "you want to go in and try making friends with the Jebusites. Just tell them Eglon sent you." The other two men snickered in the darkness.

"And if you think of running off, think again." He stood back, nocked an arrow to his bow, and waved it up the slope. "Get going."

I crawled on my belly from cover to cover; a patch of weeds here, a tumble of rocks there. I was a stone's toss from the opening when I heard a sound behind me, like a sudden, loud gulp. Then a quick clattering of stones.

Knees crashed onto my shoulder blades, pinning me to the ground. Someone grabbed a handful of my hair and yanked my head back. I heard a blade clearing its sheath, then voices above my head. They were speaking the jerky, brittle dialect of the Jebusites, but I thought I made out the words for rope and boy.

I was hauled upright, my arms clasped hard behind me. A soldier looked at me for a moment, then nodded down the slope. They took me to the place I had started from. Six more soldiers were there, and on the ground at their feet lay the old man and the two others, the gashes in their throats emptying their blood onto the ground. The legs of one of the men were still twitching.

The Jebusites argued among themselves. The one holding me wanted to kill me, I think, and the other one, the one I had seen when they pulled me to my feet, talked against it. He pointed to my ankles, where the rope burns still oozed blood. He picked up the arrow from the old man's bow and gestured with it.

One of the men, a little taller than the others, stepped up to me. He looked into my face and grabbed my chin to tilt my head this way and that. He said something to the man still pinning my arms behind me. My holder grumbled and spat, then shoved me away from him.

They made me strip off my clothes to be certain I was unarmed. When I was dressed again, four of the soldiers took me up the slope. The tall one walked beside me, gripping a handful of my clothing between my shoulder blades. When we got close to the wall, one of them called out a watchword. A gate opened just enough to let us through into the citadel.

They took me to a small wooden hut built against the wall. They put me inside and slammed the door. I heard a wooden bolt going into a hasp on the outside. The place was too low to stand, even for me. I felt my way along a wall to a corner and crouched there on my heels. I would not sit; the hut smelled of urine.

After a while the bolt slid back and the door opened. Someone stuck his head inside and gestured for me to come. I crept outside.

It was the tall man. He took me to a low building with small, barred windows high in the walls. Inside was a low table, with a few straw mats scattered on the floor. There was a lamp lit in the center of the table. He pointed at the table. I went over to it, crossed my legs and sat. He set a bowl in front of me; it was full of boiled lentils. He nodded, and I scooped the lentils into my mouth like a starving ape. They were still hot and scalded my fingers and my tongue, but I didn't care.

When I was finished he handed me a small cup of watered-down barley beer. I drank it in gulps and wiped my mouth with the back of my hand. I looked at him. He was smiling.

"Does Eglon starve his entire host this way?"

He was speaking the language of my people. Was it a trick? But his speech held none of the jitter and rush of the Jebusites. He spoke as one speaks the tongue of his birth.

"No, only the ones he conscripts from the people of Israel," I said. "His Moabites he feeds from the fat of our flocks."

He narrowed his eyes. I saw his jaw muscles working beneath his beard. "So."

He told me to sleep there. He said he would come back in the morning to find out more about Eglon and his plans.

"I hope a night's rest and a belly full of lentils doesn't dull your memory."

He went out. When the door closed, I heard a latch slide into place. I quietly tried the door, but it was locked. What else could I do except curl up on a mat and sleep?

In the morning, the tall man brought me yeast bread and cool water. After I had eaten, he said, "How long has Eglon been forcing our people into his host?"

I looked a question at him.

"Yes, I am of Israel," he said, looking away. "I came to live among the Jebusites because… it was safer for me." He looked back at me. "But why am I explaining myself to a prisoner? Come now, boy. You must tell me things my commanders will want to hear."

I told him of the conscription squads in Judah and the preparations in the camp at Bethlehem. He asked me about conditions in Judah before I was taken to the camp, and I told him about the hunger, the crippling tribute. He gripped the pommel of his sword as I spoke. I noticed he used his left hand.

"The Lord of Hosts brought us into a wide land," he said in a low voice, "but now we are penned up like cattle because we forgot his name." He stared at the tabletop.

"What?"

He shook his head. "I should be wary of letting my thoughts spill over my lips." He gave me a little, sad smile. He told me to go on, but a question was burning on my tongue.

"Who is this 'Lord of Hosts'? Is he the desert god, the one in the fire and in the cloud of dust?"

"What are you talking about?"

"Is he?"

He gave me a sideways look. "So…not everyone in Israel has forgotten the old stories."

"I don't know the stories! I don't even know the name of this god who turns his back on his people in their need."

His eyes glinted at me. He put a hand on my chest. "Be careful, boy. The Holy One is not to be tempted with hot talk. He is righteous and beyond blame. It is his people who have turned their backs."

All at once, my mother's slap was again burning my cheek. "How have you come to know so much of the gods? Have you become a priest here among the Jebusites?"

He glared at me. "There are places where loose-talking youngsters are killed for insulting men. I know what I know, boy. And you know what you know. And that is what is keeping you alive at the moment. Remember that."

I was somewhere beyond heed, beyond fear. I don't know if I was talking to him, to myself, or maybe to the no-name god. "Better a quick death here than slow starvation in Beth-Zur."

He stared at me. "Is that where you're from?"

I nodded.

"I once knew a man who spent some time in Beth-Zur. A friend. He was a lot like you: apt to speak when he should have kept still." He opened his mouth as if to say more, then stopped and looked away from me.

He got up and moved for the door. He opened it to leave, then half-turned his head toward me.

"What do they call you anyway?"

"My name is Jabez."

He stood that way for maybe ten heartbeats. Then he went out.

They kept me in the room with the barred windows for many days. The tall, left-handed man came and questioned me about the Moabites: how many I thought were in the host, what their provisioning was like, whether Eglon was with them, what kinds of weapons I'd seen in the camp. No one else ever came with him. He brought me food each time and always waited until I was finished eating before asking his questions. I found out his name was Ehud. He said it meant "strength."

Ehud was much on my mind, especially the things he said about the desert god. I thought about his anger at my words.

Something in it made me sad, rather than fearful. I felt as if I had lost something.

After a few days, I gathered enough courage to ask Ehud what his god looked like. Was he made of stone or bronze?

"The Most High has no image," he said. "He is not like anything any human has ever seen. He made everything, but he is not like anything."

"How can you sacrifice to him if he has no image? Where is his temple?"

"His Tent of Meeting is at Shiloh, in Ephraim. But the God of Israel does not live there, not really. He does not need our sacrifices. Everything is already his. When we make an offering to him, it is not because he is hungry or lonely or greedy. The sacrifice is for us, to help us remember that everything belongs to him. That the people of Israel are like nestlings in his hands. He gives us everything. He needs nothing."

Sometimes I thought Ehud was saying words that meant nothing: a god who had no house but a tent, who looked like nothing and needed nothing and had no name. A god with no shape who was more real than the figures of stone, wood, and metal. A god whose hand would sometimes injure, sometimes protect and sustain. It was hard to understand.

But other times, on my pallet at night when everything was

still, the things he told me rang inside my head like swords struck together. I tried to form in my mind a prayer to this god. But I could not think how to talk to him.

One day I asked Ehud about the fighting outside the walls. He eyed me with suspicion.

"I have friends," I said. "People like me, who were taken by force and made to do Eglon's bidding."

"Their losses have been heavy," he said finally.

"Will Jebus fall?"

He made a scoffing noise. "Not to the likes of Eglon."

"Will Jebus fight against Eglon to push him back across the Jordan?"

"A strange question for a prisoner to be asking."

I made the sign for good luck and took a deep breath. "But a question the people of Israel would still have answered."

He gave me a sharp look. Then he got up and left.

The next time he came, though, he opened the door to my cell and motioned me to follow him. "I have convinced my commander that you wish no harm to the city," he said. "I have given him my word that you are no friend of Eglon." As I started through the door, he grabbed my shoulder and brought his face close to mine. "And I will answer with my life if I am wrong," he said. "Best that you give me no reason to doubt my judgment." I nodded my understanding, and we went out.

―――――――――

The people of Jebus worshiped the morning and evening stars, Shahar and Shalem; they were twin gods with beards and pointed caps. There were also many shrines in the city to an ancient one. They called him "King of Righteousness." I couldn't learn enough of their talk to be sure if he was a man or a god.

I found out that Jebus had a protected water supply, and the fortified ridges behind the fortress guarded the fields and barns that provisioned the garrison. Any siege of this place would be long and difficult.

I had to sleep in the locked room at night, but Ehud started letting me run a few errands for him. He let me collect his rations from the city wardens and bring his food to the walls when he was on watch. Sometimes he let me hone his iron knife. He showed me how to keep the whetstone at the proper angle, how to caress the edges into keenness. He showed me how to rub it with oil and wipe it with a soft cloth before sliding it back into its sheath.

The Moabites made forays against the city off and on,

throughout the summer. In between, there would be long days of boredom. Ehud and his fellows would while away the time in gambling. Some of the others went in to the temple women or the freelance harlots in the marketplace. Everyone would grumble about having nothing to eat but lentils and weak beer. The wardens kept a tight fist on the city's larder, and hunger was still a daily companion.

Then, when an assault was mounted, fear would crackle in the air like lightning. Though I was always hurried to my cell and locked in when trouble started, I could hear the noise, the yelling. I could hear groups of men running back and forth, shouting orders. I could hear the groans of the wounded and dying. When the assault failed and the boredom returned, faces would be missing from the gambling circles. No one spoke of them, but everyone knew.

I hated being locked in during the battles. I wanted to be on the walls beside Ehud. I wanted to help him, bring water to him and the other men. Each time it happened, I measured my room countless times with my pacing. I was afraid Ehud would die and I would not be able to talk to him again. There were things I wanted to know.

I wanted to ask him why he stayed here in this hilltop city with its clatter-tongued people instead of going back to his own place. Where was his place?

One day, when I brought his rations to him, I asked him where he came from. "Gilgal, in Benjamin," he said. "My people work the stone quarries."

"Why did you leave?"

"I told you. I wasn't safe."

How could he not be safe? I saw the way the other soldiers treated him. Even his commanders asked for his word when they made their plans. Ehud had the kind of strength that doesn't need to prove itself. The kind of strength that warns others from challenge without uttering a threat or showing a fist. What could endanger such a man enough to cause him to leave the place of his own people and fight for strangers?

I looked at him and thought that if I had that kind of strength, my life would have been different. I would have given my mother a reason to do something other than weep. She would have been able to brush aside the shame everyone heaped on her. I could not help but think that her shame had something to do with me. With Ehud's kind of strength, I could have choked the shame, maybe. I could have broken down the fence it built around my mother and me. I could have fought with it. I could have sent it back to the place it came from.

CHAPTER FIVE

THE PRAYER

As the year leaned over toward the fall, the Moabite assaults became more sporadic and halfhearted. When the first rains fell, our enemies withdrew to their winter quarters near Jericho. The siege was lifted and life in Jebus became easier.

Still, I had begun to chafe at being confined. I began asking Ehud if he would not speak to his commanders for me. I told him I wanted to go back to Beth-Zur.

"What will you do there?"

"I don't know. But I am worried for my mother. I think I should go back to her."

"What about your father?"

"I have no father." I was surprised at what the words summoned in me as I stood beside the tall man who had become like my friend. Having lived for so long with the empty place where a father should have been, I did not expect the sadness to be as strong as it was in that moment.

I felt his big hand on my shoulder. "It is hard to be in a place that is not your own," he said. "Sometimes, even I…" There was a moment or two of quiet. "Maybe you will hear again of Ehud," he said finally. "When the time is right, maybe you can help me with what I have to do."

"What are you to do?"

"I don't know," he said, staring at a place just above my head. "And I don't know if you will be able to help me when I find out."

I do not think he meant for the questioning in his voice to hurt me, but it did. At that moment, I wanted more than anything to be capable of helping Ehud. But I tried to conceal my hurt. I forced a smile onto my face. "I know little of being a soldier and nothing of being a stone carver."

He grinned at me. "Maybe you know more than you think. We will see."

After a few more weeks passed, he told me he had won my release. He had spoken to the wardens, to the fathers, and to his commanders. I was free to go.

On the day of my leaving, he gave me a gourd of water and a packet of bread. And then he gave me his iron knife; I felt my eyes go wide when he handed it to me.

"This is a loan, boy," he said. "I may want this knife back someday. But you keep it for now."

He walked with me to the gate that opened on the south. "Keep the sun on your left in the morning and follow the spine of the hills," he said. "And stay away from Moabites."

He stood there until the path took me around the shoulder of the hills and hid Jebus from my sight.

―――――――――

It took me three days to walk from Jebus back to Beth-Zur. Most of the time the sky was a dirty gray and drizzled rain. The first night I was able to find a cave to sleep in. The second night I sheltered in a plum copse; the dried leaves made a softer bed than the hard clay floor of the cave, but the bare branches didn't keep off the damp so well.

It was strange to think that I desired to go back to a place that had used me the way Beth-Zur had. But the call of home can be strong, even when it calls with a crow's cackle.

When I neared Beth-Zur it was close to sundown. I decided to walk up to the Hill of Zur.

My mother was there, gripping her elbows as she faced the west. Just as I came up the rise, the sun's edge dipped below the border of the low, gray dome of cloud covering the sky. Suddenly the whole world was the color of a rose petal. I was addled by the beauty. I must have made a sound of astonishment, because my mother turned to see me standing there.

"Jabez!"

She ran to me and threw her arms around me. She was weeping. I held her. Her shoulders felt thin and brittle beneath my hands.

"I thought you must have been killed. Almost all the others—"

"I was a prisoner there," I said. "But I am home now. Things will be better."

She stepped back and looked into my face. "You are changed."

"I have been in strange places and heard words I don't understand," I said.

I looked at her. She was changed too: The creases of hunger were etched in her cheeks. Her back was more stooped than I remembered. I wished against all sense to see some release in her, some lightening of the burden she had carried all these years, of the sorrow that bound us both. But I could not find it. She saw me studying her, and she turned her face away.

"I will go down and make some bean cakes," she said. She walked past me, down the hill. I wanted to call her back. I wanted to see once more the way she had looked at me when she turned to see me standing behind her. But it was too late. She was already too far down the path. The black things circled in the air between us, and I felt a sob rising in my chest.

I turned back toward the place where she had stood. All that was left of the sun was a red-gold rim melting below the western horizon. The rose cast was fading toward purple. I walked to the spot, put my feet where her feet had been. I looked toward the west, then I closed my eyes and raised my face to the sky.

Pain was my name, and pain was the fence that closed me in. Pain was the tattered gray sky over all my days. But the rose-gold glory of the dying sun seemed to whisper something else, something I could almost, but not quite, understand. Why could I not understand? With everything in me, I longed to understand.

"Who are you?"

I shouted it at the sunset, at the dull overhanging sky. I shouted it over and over again, until my voice was tattered and raw. I fell to my knees and sobbed it into my hands. I opened my eyes. I stretched my hands toward the sky, like Raboth begging to be picked up.

Just then, the last glowing arc of the sun dropped below the rim of the world. I looked around at my feet and saw some rocks. I don't know why, but I wanted to make a marking of this place. I stacked some stones. I sat back on my heels and looked at what I had built. Was it an altar? A shrine? How did you build a shrine to something you could not see, could not even name?

I squatted there until it was full dark. I heard the trilling of one of Tubal's sons, calling a flock toward a fold in a nearby ravine. I got up and picked my way down the hill in the night.

That night I dreamed of Ehud. I was sitting with him in a small room. The images of Shahar and Shalem were in the room too, and somehow Ehud and I were shackled between them. Struggle though we might, we were securely bound. We called and shouted for help, but no one came.

"He has turned his face away," Ehud said. Tears were running down his cheeks. I was embarrassed to see such a strong man weeping like a child. "He has forgotten us, because we have forgotten him."

Then a fire was in the room. Its flames were the color of roses and I could feel the heat on my skin, but as it came nearer, I was not burned. The shackles fell away from me and Ehud and I were standing atop the walls, looking out over the Kidron Ravine, to the wide lands east of Jebus. The green hills rolled away below us, soft with the spring rains and new, tender growth. The hilltops were gently rounded, like the belly of a woman with child. It seemed to me as I looked that the land called to me with the voice of one beloved.

"This is his blessing, Jabez," Ehud said. He was laughing now. "He has remembered us, and he has delivered us from our bondage." I was laughing too, and rain was falling on our heads. We looked up at the sky and laughed as the rose-colored rain came down upon us. The voice from the green hills was like a song. I wanted to sing in answer.

I woke and lay in the quiet of everyone else's sleeping, grappling vainly for the fading tendrils of the joy I had known in the dream. Bondage, then fire, then laughing and the gentle beckoning of a bountiful country. All of it vanished into the darkness, and I felt a pang in my chest for the losing.

I got up and went outside. I walked beneath the light of the stars and thought of all the ways it is possible to hurt. I thought of the gnawing hurt in the belly that comes with hunger and the ache in the throat that comes with a hungry heart. I thought of my mother's tears. I thought of the empty place in me where a father's blessing should have been. I watched the circling of the stars, and I ached like someone aches with a soured belly. There was a void in me that fought to get out of me, but I did not know how to release that which was nothing. I wanted to tell someone, to make someone understand. I wanted more than anything to speak the hurt at the center of me and know that someone heard. I wanted to speak it to the fire in my dreams. I wanted to speak it to the Most High, the One above all naming.

My feet took me to the Hill of Zur, and I climbed it in the darkness. I found my stack of stones, and I fell to the ground beside it.

"Oh, that you would bless me!"

I cried the words into the darkness beneath the stars where I knelt. I sent them out of me, and my longing was the color of sunset on the clouds, the color of a rose.

As I had done at sunset, I raised my arms above me. How could I have known such a wish was in me? I was not certain whether I caused it to be, or whether I received it as an empty cup receives the wine poured from a pitcher.

I wanted to stretch my arms wide, to embrace the land and feel its width, its possibility. I wanted to fill it as the name of a good man fills his house, the hearts of his friends. I longed to be no more hedged about with the scorn of a community, the despite of a brother, the inconsolable grief of a mother, a father I never knew.

"Enlarge the place where I live," I said to the God of Israel. "Indeed, if you are above all gods and men as Ehud says, let me know the wideness of you. Let me pace the length and breadth you have given me, and bless you with my lips."

The thought of it caught in my throat. Between my own poverty and the expanse of the Most High was a chasm wider even than the dearest hope. It was a chasm carved by our own sins, by our shunning of the One who had brought us out of the desert, by our thoughtless harming of one another. I felt wetness at the corners of my eyes and on my cheeks. I asked for the hand of the Most High to be with me and to lift the hurt from me. I begged him to let me know but once, before I died, what it was to be free from the pain of despair. I pleaded with him to take from me the nameless reproach, the impossible, endless longing. There were so many ways to hurt. There were so many ways we could wound each other.

"Keep me from evil, that I may not cause pain."

Was I talking out loud, or was my prayer only in my head? To this day, I am not sure. But once the words were said, there was nothing else in me. I stayed beside the stones a little while longer, trying to understand what had just happened, but it was beyond me. I went back down the slope, back to my house, and tried to sleep.

———————

I knew Jashub wanted my knife. I found a smooth, palm-sized stone in a creek bed that I used to whet the edges. When I worked on it in the evenings, he watched me from the corners of his eyes. When I smoothed oil on the blade, he looked at it the way I have seen men look at a woman. He would notice me watching and quickly pretend he was doing something else. He would never ask me for it outright; he could already see the answer in my face. It would have been a shame to him to have to ask me for it, and a worse shame to have been refused. But he wanted it, just the same.

The blade was nearly as long as my forearm. I took to wearing it on a strap behind my back and beneath my clothing. Sometimes it was a little uncomfortable, but I knew there was no place I could hide it in the house without Jashub finding it. I slept with it under my pallet.

———————

The hardness of Eglon had gone on so many years that whole broods of children had been born who had never known a time of ease. Women cursed the Moabite patrols to their faces. Little boys hid behind walls and pelted them with rocks and dung. The collectors never came now without at least ten hardened fighters to protect them. Men were hiding their crops and herds in dry cisterns and caves. They were going up into the hills at night, crouching together in hidden places and plotting rebellion. I could have gone with them. My knife would have earned me welcome probably. One more weapon for the cause, and an iron blade, at that. But I never went. Neither did Jashub. He sat in the house, staring into the smoke and trying to ignore his wife and son.

While I was in Jebus, Ishma and Anani had begun finding their comfort inside a wineskin. Often enough, by nightfall they were both flat on their backs, snoring up at the roof of their lean-to. But one evening after supper I found Anani leaning against the outside wall of the house. He was rubbing his damaged right hand with his left and he was staring up at the sky.

"Come and sit down, Jabez," he said. He patted the dirt beside him.

The invitation was unusual enough to stop me in my tracks. I looked at him. Maybe it was a trick of the near-dark, but I thought a tiny smile was on his lips. I squatted beside him.

"Tell me of the war," he said. "Did you blood yourself? Did you kill your man?"

I told him I had been captured during a spying mission. I told him I had spent most of the campaign in a barred room inside the citadel.

He leaned back his head and laughed. It was not a pleasant sound.

"Locked you up like a ferret in a cage, did they?" He snickered some more. He wiped his face with the back of his ruined hand. Something about the gesture was vaguely unsettling.

"Let me tell you about my war, Jabez," he said. His head was still leaned back and his eyes were closed. His voice was low and lazy, like a man on a drowsy afternoon wondering out loud how long it will be until the next rain. "We first learned of the ambush with our noses. The smell of a thousand dead men travels a long way on the wind. We started smelling them when we were still a half-day out of camp.

"The Moabites took all our food, of course. We ate small animals we caught in the rocks. Sometimes we ate lizards and insects. The Moabites guarded the wells and springs against us, so we sucked the juice from spurges and aloes growing in the wild places. When that failed, we drank the blood of the animals we caught. Some of the men tried to drink their own urine and died."

Ishma, drawn by the sound of Anani's voice, crept out of the lean-to on all fours. He crawled down the wall to where Anani sat. He curled his legs in front of him and gripped his knees. He rocked back and forth as his brother continued talking.

"Oh, we were the brave ones when we went north, weren't we, Ishma?" Anani gave a dry chuckle and ruffled Ishma's hair. If Ishma noticed, he gave no sign. "We were going to be the hand of vengeance on Eglon for his wrongs against our kin. We were going to push him back across the Jordan." Anani shook his head. "We were fools."

He held up his mangled right hand. "Do you want to know how this happened? Do you? Well, I'll tell you anyway. You probably thought I was wounded in hand-to-hand combat, trying to escape. You probably guessed I was fighting to protect my few remaining comrades from the pursuing Moabites. Is that what you thought?" He tilted his head back and grinned. Then he looked at me. "It was a rock badger. I was trying to drag him out of his hole so I could eat him, and he nearly chewed my hand off." He cackled again, and I felt the hairs standing on the back of my neck.

"Tell me, dear brother Jabez, what was our gain for all this?" He was staring at me now, all traces of mirth gone from his face. Even the hopeless laugh was better than the expression he now wore. "Tell me. What was it? For what did I lose my hand? For what did Ishma here lose his mind? Was it for Beth-Zur? for freedom? for the love of our home, our kin?"

He grabbed a fistful of the front of my clothing. He thrust his face against mine. I could smell this morning's soured wine on his breath.

"It was for nothing." The words came out in a violent whisper. I felt his spittle hitting my face. "Nothing. All this has bought us... nothing."

I pulled his hand away and stood up. He stared at me and again the weird grin was on his face. I backed away from Anani. Beside him, Ishma still sat, rocking back and forth and staring at emptiness.

———————

Just after the spring shearing, when Jashub and I were in the market to trade for some millet seed, an old, ragged man came into the town square beside the well and rubbed dirt on his face and hands. He crawled about on his hands and knees, barking like a dog. He howled with his mouth turned up to the sky like an old, cracking bottle. He said the Great Lady of Moab was a dog who had devoured her own pups. "Is there no god in the heavens who sees the suffering of Judah?" he said. "Can the people eat sand? Can they drink the south wind?" He pounded his chest. Dust flew out from his clothing each time he struck himself.

I watched to see what Jashub would do, whether he would stand up for his god. Like everyone else, Jashub watched the old man throw dirt, listened to him bark and howl and curse the Great Lady. Like everyone else, he went on with his business when the show was over. Maybe if the Great Lady had blessed our olives more, Jashub would have felt more obligated to say something.

Another time, some men came up from Hebron. They wore robes of linen that had once been white and belts of dirty gold cloth across their chests and around their waists. Like the old man, they stood in the marketplace and harangued anyone who would listen to them.

They said they were sons of the line of Aaron the Levite who had been the first high priest of the god who brought our people out of the desert. They said the Most High had commanded them to stand in the middle of the towns of Judah and tell the people that Moab was the punishment sent by the Most High. Because the people of Judah had forgotten his name and turned their faces away from following him, the Most High had given them into the hand of Eglon of Moab, they said. After a few days of this, they left and went to some other town. Their talk did not seem to convince anyone.

Who can tell? I thought to myself in those days. If a hundred people in Beth-Zur cried out all at once to the Most High, would he move to end Eglon's cruelty? And yet, sometimes I thought a god might listen to a single voice whispering in the darkness. A god might send a dream of fire. I wanted to hope, and yet I was afraid. I wondered whether it was worse to hope, only to know the pain of disappointment. Was it better to suffer the long, numbing pain of despair? I did not know when the Most High would act. I did not know if he would heed a quiet prayer. It was too hard for me to decide.

———————

Sometimes I think lust is the only sin. Lust for a woman will make a man betray his wife, his friend, maybe even his clan. Lust for land will make him lie and murder. Lust for indulgence will make a woman sow cankers in her husband's soul. Lust for advancement and ease will make a man forget his god. There is a little god in each of our hearts that tells us we ought to have whatever it is we want. The voice of that god is very hard to ignore, even for the most righteous. It is hard to ignore because it is always telling us the thing we most want to hear.

My brother Jashub conceived lust in his heart for my iron

blade. He was not a bad man, not really. But the god inside had him by the ears and would not let him go. I had something he wanted, and he could never get that out of his mind.

It is easy enough now to see how it got its start in him. Lying on his pallet at night with Ahuzzah snoring in his ear and Raboth thrashing about in his sleep, he must have thought of the hardness of his days. His father had left him meager enough prospects, and it took all the labor he could pour into our little plots to maintain his sparse inheritance, never mind expanding it. He had two brothers who were useless to him and a third who was an embarrassment. His wife was a nag and lazy into the bargain. His stepmother, whom law and custom obligated him to care for, moved through the days like one worn out by mourning. A cloud hung over his house.

And then this humiliation of a brother comes back from a foreign place with a blade of the cherished metal of the sea people. A piece of iron like that could be traded for land. It could be traded for a ram and a brace of good ewes.

Or he could keep it in a scabbard at his side. He could walk around the village with his hand on the pommel and enjoy the eyes of the other men. He could sharpen it at night and rub it with oil. He could enjoy the feel of it in his hand, the power it gave him. One day, he could pass it on to his son. The sword of Jashub.

If I had foreseen my brother's jealousy, I would never have accepted the blade from Ehud. Or at the very least, I would have taken it back to him much sooner. And yet I cannot lie; I myself was not immune to the magic of the iron in my hand. I walked a little taller, knowing the blade was strapped on my body. I knew what iron was worth. It would have been better to take the blade into the hills and bury it. It would have been better to bury it at the top of the Hill of Zur as an offering to the Most High.

As it happened, I guess the blade became a sort of offering to him. But by then it was too late for Jashub.

CHAPTER SIX

THE BLADE

On the night of the first full moon after the beginning of the harvest the feast would begin. There would be jars from the first pressing: the clear, light oil with barely a hint of color. Someone would break a jar in the middle of the press and the music would start. In the days before Eglon, everyone would bring something—a loaf of yeast bread, a hunk of good cheese, a jar of wine, a big pot of dried dates or raisins. There would be eating and drinking and dancing as long as any of the men could hold themselves upright.

But in the Moabite times the harvest festivals were pitiful affairs. For one thing, no one wanted to show signs of plenty, since

Eglon's agents were just going to take most of it away. It's hard to feast when you know the sweat of your neck and the strength of your arms are mostly going to feed a fat king who doesn't care if you live or die. And hungry bellies do not move the feet to dance. Besides, it takes strength to feed the anger in the hearts of a down-trodden people; there is not much vigor left for celebration, nor the will to uphold it.

But the festivals went on, mostly because of custom. Some were afraid their gods would forget to send the winter rains if we didn't remind them with the feasting. Others thought the halfhearted feasting would make the gods sorry for us or jealous of the joy we should have offered them if Eglon weren't slowly starving us.

I thought many different things about the Most High in those days. Sometimes I was afraid he didn't care. Other times I per-suaded myself Ehud was right about the hard times being a just punishment for forgetting the one who brought us out of the desert. And—it pains me still to admit it—sometimes I didn't think about him at all. Sometimes we are too busy with the concerns of living to give much thought to life. I do know this: Even then, he was coming to have a place in me, though I was tending to other things. He was becoming, unfolding slowly from nothing to some-thing in my heart. I think that is his way sometimes.

Jashub and I knocked the fruit out of the year's bearing trees and gathered it into baskets. When the evenings had begun to cool, we lugged the baskets to the presses and waited while the tally men recorded our weights. The Moabite agent stood over the tally men's shoulders, with armed bodyguards close by. The oil presses were cut into the rock of a flat-topped hill on the south side of Beth-Zur. On the night of the festival, we gathered there as we always had. I expected it to be like other times since the coming of the Moabites: We would drink a little wine, then trudge back to our houses.

But when the wineskin started around, Jashub grabbed it and took several long pulls. "Hey, Jashub! Leave a little for the rest of us," one of the men said.

He wiped his mouth with the back of his hand. "Sorry, Ebal," Jashub said. "Sometimes a man needs to get the wine into him quick."

Someone brought out a shepherd's pipe and started to play, slow and soft.

"Can't you give us a fitter tune for our feast?" Jashub said. "How about something with a little life in it?" He stomped and clapped to show the pace he had in mind.

The piper shrugged and started again, a dance tune. Pretty soon some of the men were stamping their feet and bobbing their heads in time to the music.

Jashub shouted for more wine. "I thought this was a feast!"

I kept looking at him and wondering what he was celebrating that the rest of us didn't know about. But the other men seemed willing to go along with him. Why begrudge him his merriment? Morning would come soon enough.

After a while the wine started to loosen limbs and tongues. A few of the men were capering down in the press, grabbing up handfuls of the oil and smearing it on each other's faces. There was laughing and mock fighting.

"Who's got a debt?" Jashub said, yelling above the noise. "Who's got a debt?"

Was Jashub invoking the ritual of amends?

"I saw your weights this year, Jashub," one of the men said. "Have you got a bag of gold hidden somewhere beyond Eglon's reach?" When he said the name, some of the men spat. "Is that why you're acting like a moon-mad calf, pretending to be rich?"

"A debt. Who's got a debt?" Jashub just shouted louder, as if the man had said nothing.

Nobody much remembers the ritual of amends anymore. Maybe they were something our people borrowed from the people of Canaan, as we borrowed their gods. But they were always saved for the days of plenty, the fat times. The oldest man at the feast would tell of something he was owed by someone else. In the spirit of the revel, the debtor would announce to the rest how he planned to pay back the obligation. Most often the whole thing became a joke, and the object was to see who could think of the most ridiculous debt or the most hilarious repayment scheme. It was an event that ripened into the night and roared louder as the wine kept flowing.

"Well, if nobody else has a debt, then listen to me." Jashub turned and pointed at me. "Jabez, I claim amends from you."

The music died off. Everyone was watching me to see what I would do. They were watching Jashub, trying to figure out what he was thinking. I stood up. In reflex, I arched my back to feel the pressure of the blade lying along my spine.

"Jabez, I claim of you the debt of our father's honor."

If it was quiet before, it was now dead still. I think even the crickets stopped to listen.

"What are you talking about, my brother?"

"Do not call me brother." He swayed a little as he leered around at the encircling faces. "For you are not my brother. Does not everyone in Beth-Zur know that my stepmother's heart was given to another? Has not her faithlessness, suspected but never proven, risen like a stink from her since the day my father brought her under our roof?"

"That's a lie!"

"Is it? Who makes it a lie? You? You were not yet born on the day when my father spread his blanket over her, to comfort himself after the death of my mother. You didn't see the way she pined after that Benjamite when he ran away, the way she mourned him like a widow when she got the news of his death."

In the torchlight I could see the flecks of spittle in his beard. I could see his eyes rolling in his head like wet stones rolling in a cup. I knew he was drunk, yet I could not cool the fire his words kindled in my veins.

"You were not yet alive to witness the bitterness she planted in my father's heart, who wanted nothing but for her to love him as a wife should love a husband. You were not born. You could not see the slow way her cold heart killed him."

"No!" The blade was in my hand; I don't know how it got there. I leveled it at his chest. "Say you lie, Jashub. Say to these hearers that the wine is speaking, not you. Say that in your drunkenness you have slandered my mother and falsely smeared the memory of our father, and I will not cut out your heart where you stand."

"He was not your father, boy." Jashub said the words through his teeth; his fingers were curved like claws where he stood in front of me. "You are the get of a Benjamite who never knew your name."

Only when I lunged at him did I realize how he had played

me, played everyone. He was not drunk. Everything he had done had been a ploy. He knew what he meant to do, and he had guessed me from top to bottom.

He sidestepped my thrust and locked my arm in a pressure hold. He brought my wrist down across his knee once, twice. A bone snapped and I screamed. The blade clattered to the stone at the rim of the press.

I went to my knees, cradling my useless arm. Jashub picked up the blade and brandished it in the torchlight.

"Behold my payment! The just amends for the shame and bad luck this fatherless good-for-nothing and his mother have brought upon my household."

He stared around the circle of men, and one by one they looked away.

"Then let the feast continue!" Jashub said. "Where is the music? Where is the rest of the wine?"

He blared out part of a tune and cut a dance figure. His heel hit a puddle of oil, probably splashed there by the earlier romping. He lost his balance and fell backwards. He flailed his arms and spun, trying to stay upright, but he would not let go of the blade. Maybe he could not. It was beneath him when he fell. It came through his back, just below his left shoulder blade. I kept it very sharp. It killed him quickly, without a sound.

I stared at his body and at the pool of blood quickly spreading from beneath him. The blood was dark in the moonlight, almost black against the stark white stone of the press.

Some of the men made hand signs to ward off the gods of revenge. Others rushed away from the place, trying to get to their homes before the bad luck could stain them.

One of the fathers looked at me. "You are innocent of his blood, Jabez." He looked at some of the others and got their nods. "Jashub brought this on himself. But…" He pointed at the blade sprouting like a stalk from my brother's back. "I think that blade of yours is hexed now. I think you will show wisdom by taking it back to whatever place it came from. It has tasted the blood of cursing. It will drink again."

Some men went into the pit and rolled Jashub's corpse onto its side. One of them put his foot against Jashub's shoulder and pulled on the haft of the blade. It came out with a sound like a sickle going through stalks of wheat. He brought the blade to me and laid it on the stone beside me. Jashub's blood was still on it.

The ways of grief run forward and back, from side to side. They are like the cracks in the rock, like ripples in a still pool. They cover and lap each other, go around and around to make new ripples still.

If anyone thought I would rejoice at the death of Jashub, they were surprised. His strange ending brought me no joy, not even the fierce, tooth-bared joy of a wrong avenged.

After all that followed, I have sometimes wondered if the Nameless One had anything to do with Jashub's death. He is the Most High; can he not do as he likes, with one man or a thousand? But I do not like to think of him taking Jashub's life. Jashub was a poor man, a man whose hopes had been blunted so many times that he rarely raised his eyes above the level of the ground he tended. His deepest sin was resentment, but he had much to resent. If for that the Nameless One required his life of him, who can live?

Though I could not be accused of Jashub's blood, I was hardly elevated by it in the eyes of my neighbors. People stayed away from me; they made the sign against the evil eye when I came near. The men in the town square avoided me when they could. They turned their faces sideways when I spoke. When I had to trade with someone, he would not strike hands with me. I guess they thought the bad luck might jump onto them from my hands. I guess they were afraid my gaze might cause their knives to leap from their grip and gash them.

But the heaviest affliction fell on my mother. Jashub's words at the olive press ran through Beth-Zur on scores of tongues. The revival of all the old gossip tore the scabs from my mother's hurts. The pain ran through her body like poison. She was weak before. Now she was dying. I did not know if she would die in a few months or for a few years. But I knew this was her fatal wounding.

Worst for me was that in a secret corner of my mind I wondered if Jashub had spoken the truth, or part of it. What else could explain my mother's long grief? What else could justify the paused conversations, the not-quite-hidden looks? I wanted to beg her to deny it, and I loathed myself for the wanting.

CHAPTER SEVEN

THE BURDEN

My mother and I washed Jashub's body and bound it in the best linen we could afford. We put a millet cake in his mouth for the long journey to the shadow place where souls wait. I do not think I believed, even then, that the spirit of a man eats the same food as we eat, but I did not want anyone in Beth-Zur to say I had failed to show proper respect.

Any notion I had that Jashub's death would rouse Ishma and Anani from their wine-fogged despair was soon proved false. I think I would almost have welcomed their rage. As it was, they were too drunk to walk with us when we took Jashub to the tomb. I had to pay men to help me carry the body.

If the wails of a widow could carry a man's spirit to the heavens, Jashub would have rested far above the clouds. Ahuzzah blubbered and squalled on the walk to the burial caves in the hills behind the village. Her face was wet from her tears and the dripping of her nose. She tore her robe. She stopped every four or five steps to scoop up a handful of dust to throw upon her head. She prostrated herself on the ground and moaned; we had to stop and wait for her.

I felt sorry for Raboth; he watched his mother with big, scared eyes. Bad enough to have lost his father before his tenth winter, but now I think he feared his mother's mind had flown, as well. He carried his father's squat, cup-shaped god. He held it in front of him like an offering or a shield. Maybe he thought whatever had made his father lie without moving had also made his mother crazy. Maybe he was afraid it would come after him, too.

A ravine west of Beth-Zur led to the place of the caves. The path brought us in along the floor of the ravine, and the burial caves stared out from the bleached stone of the hillside above like blind eye sockets. We climbed the zigzag path up to the grottoes. Friends or family members of the dead ones had traced god-symbols on the outside of some of the entrances. Some of the pictures looked black and crusted, as if someone had dipped a brush or a chewed twig in blood and daubed the stone with it. Some of them were scratched into the stone. There were pictures of the dead ones, working or praying or lying with their mates. There were pictures of their families mourning them. There were pictures of the gods receiving the many offerings the dead ones had made during their lives.

We laid Jashub's body on a stone shelf inside the cave. One of the carriers brought out a pigeon and pulled its head off. He sprinkled the blood on Jashub's head and feet. Raboth handed the god image to his mother and Ahuzzah set it on Jashub's chest, crying and blubbering all the while. The man squeezed a few drops of the pigeon's blood into the bowl in the Great Lady's lap. We backed out. Raboth and the women went back to the house while the other men and I stacked stones in the opening to keep out the jackals and the wild dogs.

I thought about Jashub, lying there in the darkness with the Great Lady on his chest. For days and nights he would lie there; the sun's coursings would swing to the north and then back to the south in its annual crossing. The moon would wax and wane countless times. And still he would lie there. He would lie there until the flesh of his chest caved in and his limbs dried into wrinkled sticks, until the blackened lips pulled back from his teeth. He would grin his death-grin up at the ceiling of the cave. Maybe the Great Lady would tumble off his chest to lie on the cave floor in the dark, and who would know?

Would his soul, the breath of him, stay in the cave with his body? Would that which made him Jashub go on? Would it sit in the bowl of the Great Lady, sit like an offering of oil or beef fat that glazes and turns rancid after a few days? What note would she take of it? What comfort would she offer Jashub for all the oil he had rubbed on her and all the pieces of meat he had placed in the bowl on her lap?

Did the gods care about the death of humans? I wondered what a human soul looked like. When we die, I thought, do our souls exit through our mouths? our eyes? Or do they leak out through our pores, as the water in us leaks out on a hot day? I could not think of an image for my soul. I could not think of myself dead, as Jashub was dead. My spirit was as featureless and unthinkable to me as the face of the Nameless One. If I could know what he looked like, maybe I could know about my soul. Maybe he held the answers. Maybe he collected the souls of all those who died and held them for some purpose of his own. I tried to say a prayer to him for my soul, for the soul of Jashub. I could not think of anything to say; everything that came into my mind seemed either too much or too little.

I did not know how to speak to him. I thought of my cry on the hilltop, the words that had tumbled into my mind and from my lips later that night, beside the pile of stones. The words that almost seemed to come from somewhere else and from me at the same time.

Could a god know a man like that? Could a god be so close that his thoughts seemed like the man's own thoughts, yet not the man's? Could a god move within a man as his own spirit moved within him? Could one so mighty be at the same time so close and unsuspected? Maybe that was why my people had turned away from the Most High. Maybe they had simply overlooked him. The thought of it made me afraid.

───

I bore the encumbrance of the household now, but not its headship. That was in the hands of Anani, who spent his days scheming to get another bellyful of wine and his nights sleeping off its effects. It was easy to see that if I left matters to him, we would starve even quicker than Eglon might wish. I decided to go forward as if I had the right to do what I thought was best. If Anani cared enough about exercising his birthright to shake off his sloth, so much the better. But until then, someone had to figure out a way to keep us fed.

I don't know what Ahuzzah expected at my hands. Maybe she thought I would take my revenge for her mistrust of me, for the evil she had spoken of me to Jashub. Half the time she looked at me like dung on her shoe, and the other half she watched me as one thief watches another.

I told her she need not worry. I told her I would do every duty owed a brother's wife. I told her I would protect her son like my own blood. And then I told her she would have to take on more of the household tasks, since my mother was getting older and weaker.

She wanted to know what I meant by "more." I told her she would have to grind the grain, bake the bread, keep the water urns full, and tend her son until he was old enough to go to the fields with me. She looked at my mother, lying on her pallet, and said she didn't see why Mother Libnah couldn't at least do the baking.

I think I let my irritation show in my voice. I told her she would do as I said, and that if she didn't like the duties I gave her she was free to take it up with Anani, or the fathers, for all I cared. She rolled her eyes and flopped down on her mat. But when I came back from the field that evening, she had made bread. I do not say that it was tasty, but it was bread.

After Eglon's men took what they wanted that year, we had just enough of the poorer grade of oil to keep us until the next harvest, if we were careful. My mother told me she would keep the lamps trimmed and in good order. That was an easy enough thing for her to manage, she thought. That, and maybe a little of the cleaning, she said.

Everyone in Beth-Zur was planting lentils in those days. One of the men had said he'd heard Eglon couldn't abide the taste of lentils, so everyone wanted to grow nothing but. The king still took them for his armies and his servants, but it gave us a little twinge of pleasure to know his paunch wasn't expanding because of our labor. Or if it was, he wasn't enjoying it.

In another season or two I started taking Raboth to the field with me. For a while it was more trouble than doing the work alone. One day, I think he plucked up a whole row of good plants before I noticed what he was doing and showed him the difference between a lentil and a weed. Another time I had to stop him from chasing a curlew. He was trampling all across the crop trying to jump on the long-legged bird that kept itself always just out of his reach.

He was willing to learn though. After a while I started to think I didn't mind his company so much. And he seemed to like being with me well enough.

His head was full of questions like a dog's hide is full of ticks. "Uncle, why are a goat's droppings different from a cow's?"

"Uncle, how did old Tubal get to be so rich?" "Uncle, where does the sun go at night?" "Uncle, why does a donkey stand when it sleeps?"

He had a ferret's curiosity and its energy, this tousle-headed, sunburnt son of my brother. He tumbled about me like a rag ball with legs, bouncing against my shins and bounding away, blown back toward me on the wind then off again, turning over rocks and pulling branches off trees and peering down holes in the ground. I could not understand how my dour brother and his sluggish wife had made such a thing between them.

"Uncle, did you hate my father?" he asked me one day.

We were plucking the dried pods from the lentil stalks and tossing them in baskets. I gave him a sharp look, but he was turned away from me, busy with the row he was straddling as he picked.

"No, I did not hate him," I said. "He was my brother."

"Mother told me you did."

"She is… mistaken."

"I thought so."

He said it with the same voice he might have used if I had asked him to fetch something for me.

"No matter what anyone says, Raboth, I wished no harm to your father. It is a very bad thing to want to hurt someone in your own household."

"Why?"

"Because it is the duty of blood to look after blood. Because a man must be able to trust those who share the place where he sleeps. Because one who does not regard his own clan is cursed. Because… because the gods say it must be so."

"Which gods?"

The ones this boy should be questioning instead of me. "There are many things about the gods I do not understand, Raboth."

"Are there many of them?"

"I don't know. Some people say so. Some people say there is only one god. Or maybe they say this god is stronger than all the others."

"Which is it, Uncle?"

I straightened and stared at the pods in my hand. I thumbed one of them open to look at the lentils lying inside, rusty green pebbles in a dimpled bed.

"I believe there is one God. I believe it is so." I tossed the pods in my basket and bent again to my work.

"What is your god called?"

I laughed when he asked it. I don't know why. This reed-voiced boy wore me out with questions, tied them on my arms one after another, like stones in a net, and now he asked me the question of all questions, the single question I would have most liked to answer. Maybe I laughed at the great joke in it. Maybe I laughed to keep from sobbing.

═══════════

The old woman Gedilah died that winter. My mother noticed that for several days in a row, no smoke came out of the hole in the roof of her shack, just down the path from our house. We went there and pulled aside the door covering and found her on her mat. She was very stiff; we had some work binding the corpse. I was glad it was not summer.

My mother went to the fathers and asked for a place to bury her. They gave Gedilah a shallow cleft in the lower part of the caves. We laid her there and blocked the opening with stones as best we could. I thought about the stories and half-stories she told about the Nameless One. I wondered if that was enough to cause him to take notice of her. I wondered if he would protect her flesh from the night creatures. It was not a very good tomb.

═══════════

The iron blade hung on its strap from a peg in the roof beam above the place where I rolled out my mat and slept. I didn't bother to hide it anymore. No one else in the house—indeed, in all of Beth-Zur—would touch it or look at it. Raboth was even afraid to ask me questions about it.

I didn't know what to do with it. It was too valuable to throw away, but it was too dangerous to keep. It pressed on me like a loaded pack presses on the shoulders of a man who has been walking all day. I had dreams about it. Sometimes in the night, I thought my brother's blood dripped from it onto my face.

Perhaps I needed to make the journey back to Jebus to return it to Ehud. But how did I know he was there still? If I left, who would take care of my mother and Raboth? Who would watch to make sure Ahuzzah didn't neglect her chores?

To escape my troubling thoughts, I poured my attentions into my work. The land was my only comfort, and it was a hard comfort, bought with sweat and aching muscles at the end of each day. I rose early and toiled until I could barely see my hand in front of my face. I dug around the trees and pruned their branches. I weeded the field and turned the soil with my mattock. I pried up rocks and stacked them around the edges of the field. In the dry times, I carried water in hide buckets from the springs in the hills.

Slowly, I started to see the land yield to my attentions. The trees became more productive. My grain harvest improved a little from year to year. Some of my neighbors started to notice. They started to watch what I was doing. They started to talk to me in the square, instead of avoiding me. They even started to ask my advice sometimes. Hard work is something all people of the land understand and respect, whatever else they may think of you.

And then, the day came when everything started to change at once. I knew it when I heard his voice, calling to me from the road as I was grafting sprigs among the olive trees. Before I turned around to see him, I knew.

"Jabez! Won't you greet me? I've come to ask for your help."

It was Ehud.

CHAPTER EIGHT

THE MUSTER

H e had left Jebus three days before, Ehud said. He had come straight to Beth-Zur to see me before doing anything else. I gave him a strange look. What was so important about me, I asked, that it should draw him down from the safety of Jebus and its walled fortress?

"I was hoping you could tell me," he said. There was a strange light in his eyes as he spoke. I felt a quick thrill of alarm, or maybe it was excitement.

It was cold that day. We went into the house. Ishma and Anani were lying by the firepit. Anani opened one eye at Ehud when we came in. "Did he bring anything to drink?" Ehud looked a question at me. I shrugged.

We sat down. There was more gray in his beard than I remembered. But he still had the same tall form, the same strong shoulders. His eyes roved the dim, smoky room. Ahuzzah sat in one corner, wearing her usual sulk as she scraped burnt leavings from a pot. Raboth was near her, staring at the tall stranger and plainly thinking of the first dozen questions he would ask as soon as he could. My mother lay on her mat with her face to the far wall. Her cloak was pulled over her. Her shoulders rose and fell in a slow, steady rhythm.

Ehud turned toward me. "The Most High has called me to raise up Judah and Benjamin to cast off the yoke of Eglon," he said. He leaned in and put his hand on my knee. "He has heard the cries of his people, Jabez. His compassion is aroused. It is time."

I could see Ahuzzah turning her head, trying to listen without seeming to listen. I put my face closer to Ehud's. "What do you mean? I have seen no one making offerings to him. I have heard no one calling on him in the marketplace. How do you know this?"

"Because he has told me." The light was in his eyes again, strange and fearful and thrilling. "He is the mighty one, Jabez. One man is an army if the Most High fights with him."

I have seen the secret ceremonies in the fall, when men drink and dance themselves into a frenzy to attract the attentions of the Great Lady. I have seen their faces, flushed with spiced beer and the madness of the god, kissing and embracing the ground as if it were a woman. I have heard them shout, heard the oaths they have made to the god; I have seen them swear by the blood of their sons to honor the Great Lady, to feed her and revere her if only she will send forth the fruit of her womb once again.

But I had never heard anything like the sound of Ehud's voice. He made no oaths, spoke hardly any words, yet certainty burned in him, made his face shine like the face of one of the sons of heaven. I was afraid of him and drawn to him. I was a moth in the glow that came from him. My mouth went dry.

"What will you do? Tell me and…I will help if I can."

He gripped my wrist with his left hand. "Tell the men of Beth-Zur to gather in a secret place. Let me speak to them. Let me tell them of this thing the Most High is getting ready to do. Let me call them to his side."

There was a rustling on the other side of the room. My mother was sitting up, looking at Ehud. It was not proper for a woman to stare at the face of an unknown man. I felt my cheeks beginning to burn with embarrassment.

"You are a Benjamite," she said. "I can hear it in your accent."

Ehud nodded. He looked at me for an explanation. I could not meet his eyes.

―――――――

The cave where the men gathered was in a small blind canyon. Walking along the floor of the gully, I could sometimes hear stones clicking together in the rocks above us. I knew that if I hadn't been recognized by the watchers, Ehud and I would already have arrows in our throats.

The opening was partly hidden behind a thicket of scrub juniper, situated so that you had to know exactly where to look for it. As we parted the boughs of the trees, we could see a dim glow from back in the cave. A shadow separated from the darkness as we came through the junipers.

"This man is under the protection of my roof, and no foe," I said.

The guard stepped aside. We went into the cave.

About twenty men sat in a loose circle around a single lamp with three wicks. Some of the fathers were there. One of them spoke as we came in.

"Jabez, you have not been here before. Why now? And who is this foreigner you bring into our midst?"

I could feel their eyes on me, on Ehud, looming behind me. "You all know me," I said. "You know I've lived here with you, since the day I was born. You know my mother and my father."

I watched their eyes when I said it. Some of them looked away.

"For most of my life Eglon of Moab has had his foot on our necks," I said. "For several years now you have been coming up here at night to talk about war, about taking back the freedom we used to know. Now I have brought this man to talk to you. He is a guest in my house. He is a fighter from Jebus, a city that has not bowed its knee to Moab."

There was a rustle of murmurs at this.

"Why should we listen to a foreigner?" someone said. "What gives him the right to tell us something, just because he comes from a walled town on a hilltop?"

"I am a Benjamite," Ehud said, stepping in front of me. "My people are from Gilgal, almost within sight of Eglon's summer palace in Jericho. We bore the brunt of his cruelty when he came across the Jordan. His commanders eat the dates from our groves and take their pleasure with our women. I have no love for anything of Moab."

"Well, we share that, at least," one of the fathers said into the silence. "But Eglon's armies are hardened in battle. With what he plundered from us, he has gotten chariots and spears and swords of iron. What has changed, that we should now follow a Benjamite against him?"

Some of the younger men made disgusted sounds and looked away. Others nodded. All of them listened to hear what Ehud would say. He waited, let the quiet get heavier and heavier. He looked at them like a man measures a piece of ground.

"The Most High, the God of Abraham, Isaac, and Jacob, the one who brought our people through the desert in fire and cloud—he has seen the distress of his people at the hands of Eglon. He has put his spirit upon me and called me to put an end to the Moabite oppression. And now with my voice he calls to you and says, 'Return to me, people of Judah, and I will heal your land.'"

Some of the older men flinched when Ehud named the names of the ancient ones; most of the rest only looked puzzled.

"What god is this, that we should trust him on your word?" someone said.

"Who is the Great Lady of Moab, and what has she done for you, that you should continue to trust her?" Ehud said.

Some of them made the crossed-finger sign for protection.

"It is because you have turned aside to other gods that the Most High has allowed Eglon to torment you for all these years," Ehud said. "If the Great Lady has ears, if she has any strength to act, let her hear me now and strike me where I stand."

Their eyes grew wide at this. The ones closest to him scooted away, looking around as if they heard a noise of danger out in the night.

Ehud stood watching them and started to smile. Then he started to laugh. The sound was strange and frightening in the yellow-flickering dark. I was afraid for him, but proud of him too. I wanted to sing a fierce song. I wanted to do something bold and immediate.

"Men of Beth-Zur," he said, "I will tell you this: The Most High will smite Eglon. The king of Moab will die and his flocks will be scattered. In that day, will you stand with me and with the God of Israel, or will you still be hunkered in this cave, talking about what you would do?"

The light in him was starting to kindle in the eyes of some of them. I could see them rubbing the hafts of their blades and thinking about what they had heard. I could see Ehud's avowal working in them, introducing them to a new and unfamiliar hope.

In the days that followed, men were in and out of our house almost constantly. They came in twos and threes, and they wanted to talk to Ehud. Some of them were from towns several days away. Some of them had strange accents. They wanted to know what he knew about the disposition of Eglon's troops, about where they might lay hands on weaponry. They wanted to know about this god whom Ehud assured them would fight for them against the hosts of Moab. Even the fathers came, eventually. They listened to him and rubbed their beards. They looked at each other and nodded.

I began to acquire a sort of reflected fame. People finally began asking me about my time in Jebus: what I had seen there, how the people of that city conducted warfare, whether I thought they would join the uprising against Eglon. They asked me about Ehud. They wanted to know if I had ever seen him fight. I told them he saved me from a whole group of men who wanted to kill me. I let them think of it as they might.

The quiet urgency of those days seeped even through the besotted cloud in which Ishma and Anani lived. When men came to meet with Ehud, I saw them watching from the doorway of their lean-to. I saw them talking to each other and looking at Ehud, at me. I thought it might be a good thing. I thought maybe at last they were deciding to come out of the place they were hiding. I should have seen the danger in it, but I didn't.

My mother studied Ehud when she thought no one was looking. Whenever he came near her I could see her change, become attentive. Once, when she was trimming the wicks near where he was sitting, I saw her eyes flicker back and forth from his face to her work. She was smiling to herself, like someone remembering a favorite song from a better time. I could not think of the last time I had seen her smile, and the sight of it now shamed me. If I knew the words to stop her that wouldn't have torn out my own heart, I would have said them. I lived in dread that someone else would notice the way she looked at him. My old shame rose up in me, whispered hateful words in my head. *The get of a Benjamite who never knew your name...*

Spring came and one night I couldn't sleep. I got up from my mat and the iron blade swung in front of my eyes on its strap. I looked at it a long time. I took it down from the peg and went outside. I climbed the stairs to the roof. I lay on my back and looked up at the stars, thinking of the pale green shoots bursting through my field's warm ground. The winter rains had been good. The olive trees had many clusters of small, white blossoms that would become fruit as the days lengthened into summer. I looked at the clusters of stars and thought of the clusters of olive blossoms, and I wondered if I would be alive at the end of the summer to gather the fruit and take it to the presses on the hillside.

The season for war was near. I did not know how much of the fight the Most High would take upon himself, but I thought there would likely be some of it left over for the men of Judah and Benjamin. I did not know how many of the Moabites' arrows and blades the Most High would turn aside. I trusted Ehud and I was trying to trust the Most High, but still I could not help thinking of what it might feel like to die. I had the iron blade lying beside me. I ran my hand along the flat of the blade and I looked at the stars and tried to count them. I tried not to be afraid.

I heard footsteps coming up the stairs. It was Ehud. He came over and sat beside me.

"I just came back from talking to some of the men. Your mother told me you came up here."

He was looking at me, but I kept my eye on a star with a reddish tinge, riding low in the western sky.

"I have never asked you…what is her name?"

I felt the weight of dread settle suddenly on me. "Whose name?"

"Your mother."

"Why do you want to know?"

He looked at me in surprise. "My question is not impolite, is it?"

"No… I'm sorry. Her name is Libnah. It means—"

"Brightness. I know."

I looked at him, but his face was turned away. He was thinking about something for a long time.

"What is it?" I said.

He pulled his attention back to me. "Oh…probably nothing that would mean anything to you."

We sat in silence for a while. I picked up the blade.

"When you go north to Gilgal, will you take this blade with you?" I handed it to him.

"This is the one I gave you."

"Yes."

"Does it not please you?"

In slow words I told him of my brother's death. I told him about the dreams, about the words of the father that night at the presses. "I don't want it anymore. You need to do some killing. You take it back."

He sat quiet for a long time. He picked up the blade and hefted it, felt its balance. He cut through the air with it.

"A good blade," he said.

"It does not fit my hand as well as a mattock."

"Will you use your mattock against the Moabites?"

"If I have to."

He was looking at me again. "You are a good man, Jabez. An honest man. One who wishes no harm."

The red star was just beneath the clump of stars that stood for Shalem and Shahar, the twin gods of Jebus. It was about to fall below the shoulders of the hills. I sat up and looked at him.

"Too bad wishing no harm doesn't keep you from harm."

"Are you afraid?"

I looked away from him. I nodded.

"Then you are like every good soldier I have ever met." He rubbed the blade on his sleeve and held it up in the star-shine. "A man who goes into battle without fear tickling his gut is a fool, and one about to die, most likely." I felt his hand on my shoulder. "I'm going down now."

He walked across the roof and down the stairs. "I can't sleep with all these stars staring at me," he said. I waved at him and lay back down. The red star was gone now.

Then I heard the strangled cry and the sounds of struggle. I heard the dull sound of a fist striking flesh. I jumped up and ran to the stairs.

Below, at the corner of the house, Ehud was struggling between two figures. The three of them grunted and growled like fighting beasts. One of the attackers had Ehud's arms pinned behind him and the other was trying to come at him with a blade of some kind. But Ehud was kicking and slinging himself about, using his holder for balance as he fended off the other with his feet. There were gashes in his calves, but still he kicked and tried to free himself.

I ran down the stairs, feeling my bladder release in a warm

flood down my legs. I threw myself at the legs of the man holding Ehud and the three of us went down in a tangle. I looked up in time to see the other attacker's blade arcing toward me. I grabbed his wrist and forced the blade enough to one side to miss my chest, but I felt it slice through the meat of my upper arm. I think I must have let out a cry of pain, but I don't remember for sure.

Ehud was able to free his left hand and the iron blade flashed in the starlight. The man who had been holding him groaned and lay still. The other man ran off into the night, crying like a woman.

That was when I realized who the attackers were.

I bent to the man on the ground. Anani gasped and held his middle, but blood flowed around his fingers like a stream in freshet. I got my arms under his shoulders.

"Why, Anani? This man was our guest. He offered you no harm."

"War… gains… nothing," Anani said in a voice like a jackdaw's croak. Then his head lolled back and he died.

We found Ishma the next day, sprawled with a broken neck at the foot of a gorge in the hills. He still held the knife in his hand.

CHAPTER NINE

THE BATTLE

Again my mother and I made bodies ready for burial. Again we made the slow walk to the caves. This time, though, Raboth was old enough to help carry his uncles. His face was still as we laid Ishma and Anani to rest. He did not ask me any questions. I would not have known what to say to him if he had.

Most of the village thought their deaths were no more than they deserved. After all, hadn't they struck at the man who was becoming widely known as the deliverer of our land?

But I could not dismiss them so lightly. My mother could not. Had she not cared for them when they were young, before war and wine ruined them? I watched the sorrow deepen in her, pull her farther down. I saw her drowning in it, and I feared her time was not long.

―――――――――

A plan had emerged. At harvest time, when the tribute was gathered to take to Eglon in Jericho, Ehud would take the place of one of the fathers, going with the levy for Beth-Zur. He was too well known in the territory of Benjamin, he said. The Moabite commanders overseeing Benjamin had a number of especially good reasons to remember him, he said. So, he would go with the train from Beth-Zur.

Once the tribute was on the way to Jericho, the men of Beth-Zur and the surrounding towns were to go up near Gilgal. We were to move at night, in small groups. We were to gather just north of Gilgal, in the edge of the territory of Ephraim, and wait for the sign. There would be other fighters to help us, Ehud said. The men of Benjamin were mustering, and a few men from the southern parts of Ephraim.

"What will the sign be?" everyone wanted to know. But Ehud said the Most High had not yet shown him. When it came, he said, we would know.

By this time, every man in Beth-Zur had fashioned one or two weapons for himself. Sickles were heated and straightened into rude swords. Poles of oak and ash were sharpened, the points hardened in fire. I put a decent edge on my mattock and wrapped the haft with strips of bronze for strength.

Raboth followed me around like a puppy. No, he was too young to go north with the fighting men, I told him. No, we would not be using boys for spies, no matter how well they might fit into small spaces. No, I had no intention of being killed. I tried hard to sound convincing.

"Uncle, I don't know how to take care of the land."

I grabbed his shoulders and looked at him. "Have you been following me around all these years and getting in my way and asking me a hundred questions a day without learning anything? Maybe you know more than you think."

I had to smile. "You will do well. The land will tell you what it needs, if you will just listen. And I won't be gone that long anyway, maybe."

He grabbed me around the waist and buried his face in my robe. I held him, trying to blink back the water gathering in my eyes.

⸻

The Moabite agents came, driving the creaking oxwains that would haul back to Jericho the tribute for fat Eglon. We watched the wains being loaded out under the stern gaze of the Moabite soldiers, each of us wondering if we would soon be facing this man or that in battle. I looked at their swords, their iron-butted spears, and cried out silently to the Nameless One. I hoped Ehud's sending was true. I hoped the sign, when it came, was sure.

It was a time of hidden farewells. In their houses at night, men held their wives as if they might never hold them again. On the walk north, I heard my neighbors tell of it with their voices catching in their throats. A man would come around a corner and see his children playing in the dust and he would suddenly have to weep. Another man would remember he owed his neighbor a hin of grain and go immediately to repay it. This was nothing like the comical ritual of amends. This was the grim-faced dealing of those who wanted all their accounts settled. Who knew which of us would fall and which would come back? Who knew if any of us would come back?

―――――――――――

The heat of full summer descended as the last of the wains rolled out of Beth-Zur toward the north, Ehud with them. I was glad the rest of us were traveling at night. The skies during the day were lids of brass on the cauldron of the land. Even at night, the rocks held the heat of the sun. But at least there were breezes sometimes.

We marched north through the gullies and the ravines and tried to find a cave or some thick foliage to lie in during the day. Our weapons were bound in cloth to keep them quiet. We drank from the springs and pools we passed; we stayed away from towns. We passed by Etam and made a wide circuit around Bethlehem since there was still a Moabite camp there. We kept the high reach of Jebus on our left as we passed it. We hoped the men of Jebus would come out and fight our common enemy, once things got started.

We came out into the flat country along the river just west of Beth-hoglah, in Benjamin. Another night's march through the dense thickets and soggy terrain of the Jordan and we came out above Gilgal, to the high place of Seirah in Ephraim.

Many men were there ahead of us; we were glad of it. They were camped in every scrap of cover the broken country could afford. There were men in every cave, every hollow in the rocks. We hid ourselves in copses. Some of us slept in trees. We were no more than a half-day's march north of Jericho; to this day I do not know how we avoided Eglon's notice, unless the Most High spread his cloak over us and hid us from Moabite eyes. If our encampment had gone on for more than the day or two it did, surely they would have discovered us. But they didn't.

———————

Many stories have been told of how Ehud delivered Moab into our hands that day. I have heard men tell that Eglon knew him when he saw him, that they fought hand-to-hand for a whole morning before Ehud was able to kill him. I have heard others say that the fire of the Most High came out of Ehud, that the sword he buried in Eglon's belly was red hot. I do not know how such wild tales get started.

The truth is, Ehud appealed to two things no king can resist: gold and the words of the gods. He told Eglon he knew of a place where secret gold was buried and the king wanted no one else to hear. Ehud told him it was a secret that came from the Most High God. Kings like to hear from the gods. They are used to important news from important places. They expect special privileges. Ehud said what he knew Eglon would want to hear.

I wonder if Eglon's eyes were upon Ehud when he stabbed him. I know that blade; it can kill silently. I wonder if the king made a sound as he died.

Ehud left the king bleeding on the floor of his palace and

slipped out as quietly as a mother leaves a sleeping child. He rode north to the place where we were waiting and blew the rams' horns. When we saw him there was no doubt in anyone's mind that the sign had come.

He was standing on a huge rock near the center of the camp. "The Most High God has given your enemies into your hands!" he said. The sun was behind him; the light gave him an aura like one of the heavenly beings. He thrust his left fist in the air and it was still coated with the blood of Eglon. His arm was covered with it halfway to his elbow. We cheered our throats raw. The blood in our veins was as hot as the sun.

We rushed down from the high place of Seirah toward the fords of the Jordan. The hosts of Moab were in complete disarray; maybe the Nameless One put a spirit of confusion into them. Maybe the death of their king made them think their gods had abandoned them. They came in disorder, like bandits fleeing pursuit. They were tripping over each other in their haste. In the hubbub and tangle they cut and slashed at each other. We tumbled boulders onto their heads as they tried to cross the river. We killed them with stones from slings, with our sharpened sticks. We went among the slain and took their weapons to use against their fellows. They fell like wheat before us. I grew sick with the killing.

Some think it was all over in one day, that we cut down the

army of Moab like a ripened field and that was the end of it. We killed a great many Moabites that first day, it is true. But there was more killing to be done.

Now that I am old, those days are harder to think about. I know that it had to be done, and I know that we could never have overcome the armies of Moab if the Most High had not been with us. Still, I now understand more about how easy it was for Ishma and Anani to numb themselves with drink. After all these years, I am still sorry for the mothers and wives in Moab who never saw the return of their loved ones. I wish there had been another way. But sometimes blood is the only thing that will do. I do not understand this, but I think it must be so.

We dragged bodies out of the Jordan for days. There were too many of them to bury; we piled faggots of wood all about them and burned them. The smoke billowed black into the sky, like an offering. I wonder if the smell of it pleased the Most High. I wonder if the smoke made his eyes smart, as it did mine.

━━━━━━━━━

The dancing in the streets of Jericho went on for several days. The poor of the city were allowed into the summer palace. They carried off all of Eglon's perfumes and precious woods, his ebony and ivory-inlaid furnishings and his fine linens.

I found Ehud in the courtyard of the summer palace, giving directions to the men from the different towns about redistributing the foodstuffs in Eglon's storehouses. I told him I was going back to Beth-Zur with the wains.

"I will come to you when I have finished my business here," he said.

I told him he would always be welcome in my house. We parted, and the crowd closed around him. I did not expect to see him again, with all he had to do. I was proud to have known him.

We took the wains to the storehouses and loaded them with grain and oil. We loaded casks of dates and dried figs, bushels of almonds. We broke vials of oil over the heads of the oxen as we started south out of Jericho, back to the towns of Judah.

What a procession we made, dancing and laughing and singing as we walked beside the plodding oxen! In every town along the road, women and children came out to sing and dance with us. When we came to a town where any of us lived, we would unload grain and oil and dried fruit and almonds. The people would make us stay with them for a meal. They would make us tell stories of the battle, of the death of the hated Eglon. They would make us tally up the slain for them. The numbers grew with each telling, and Ehud became mightier and holier. All of us grew taller. We became the brave men of Gilgal.

I did not feel like a brave man. I only wanted to get back to Beth-Zur to see how my field was doing. I wondered if Raboth had remembered to water the trees. I wondered if he had remembered to store the grain up out of the wet. I wondered if he had kept out enough seed for the next sowing time.

When we finally turned aside at Beth-Zur, I was completely weary of the celebration. I was tired of telling about killing Moabites, I was tired of recounting Ehud's speech before the battle, I was sick to death of making it all sound better than it really was. Everyone knew that it was my blade that Ehud had used to kill the king, and some wanted me to talk about that.

I didn't want to talk about it. I just wanted to get back to my house and my family and my land and my life. I wanted quiet, and a chance to rest. I wanted to sit at the crest of the Hill of Zur at sunset and think about many things.

When I saw Raboth at the side of the road he was crying. I went to him and put my arms around him.

"What's the matter, boy? I'm back, just as I said."

"I'm not weeping for you, Uncle," he said. "It's Grandmother. She's dying."

I knew she was dying. She had been dying all my life, I think, and faster since that night at the olive presses. But still I was unprepared for what I saw when I walked in the doorway of the house.

Her body was a bundle of sticks inside her clothing. Her eyes peered out through tunnels. The skin of her face was stretched, the color of old tallow. I kneeled beside her and took her hand.

"Mother. I have come home."

"Jabez." Her voice was a fading whisper. "A brave man of war. How I wish your father could see you now. He would change his mind surely."

I did not know what to think. Her words stabbed me like no Moabite spear could have. For an awful moment, I had the thought of shaking her, making her tell the truth of my birth before she went into the place of shadows and waiting. But her eyes had closed. She had retreated from me. Only the slight movement of her breastbone showed she was still alive.

For all the rest of that day I sat beside her, and all that night and the next day. I sat there as long I could hold myself awake.

People brought things into the house: jars of figs and dates from the wains, baskets of grain, skins of wine, cheeses wrapped in linen cloth. I saw none of it, barely heard it. My eyes were on her face, my ears attuned only to the slight sound of her breathing.

Please do not leave yet. Please do not die without giving me your blessing. I had no father's blessing; do not make me live with nothing but memories of you and regrets for what I do not know...

I must have fallen asleep by her pallet. One moment I was holding her hand, silently pleading, and the next I was standing on the top of the Hill of Zur. The sun was setting beneath a long bank of clouds, and the world was again the color of a rose's heart. And then, The Voice came.

CHAPTER TEN

THE BLESSING

I n my dream, I fell to the ground. I wept for the mere sound of it, like all the oceans and winds of the world, gathered together inside my head. I was afraid I would die with the terror of it, the beauty of it. I knew I would die. And I knew it would be worth death, and more, to hear what I now heard. I stretched myself on the ground like a defeated man. I waited for the stroke that would destroy me, even as the utter love, the breathtaking power of the speaking ravished my soul.

I have remembered you.

The words were live coals in my ears. Remembered me? For what? There was nothing in me worth remembering, nothing that deserved even the tiniest corner of the glory that now poured through me like a flood of molten gold.

You will not be forgotten. No more shall you be known as "Pain." Your name shall be a word of blessing to many, to generations yet unborn.

Is there in the tongues of men a song that is equal parts shame and glory? If there is, it is that song that now broke open inside my soul. That I, who had never known my father or the love of my brothers, should be thought of at all by those yet to come, much less remembered kindly—it was too much. I could not contain it.

I have heard your prayer, the requests you have placed before me. Arise now, and see how I will do what you have asked.

The glory left me. In my dream, I lay on the hillside and sobbed, I don't know how long. My face was wet from my tears, it was crusted with dirt. I rolled onto my back and covered my face with my hands. I was weeping for the joy of what I had heard. I was weeping because the dreadful beauty had gone up from me, and I thought I would die from the emptiness.

Someone was shaking my shoulder. I opened my eyes and saw, not the sky above the Hill of Zur, but Ahuzzah, leaning over me. There was something like concern in her face.

"Someone is here to see you," she said.

I wiped my face and sat up. Ehud stood in front of me. I blinked at him. I looked at my mother. Still her chest rose and fell in short, broken movements.

Ehud held out his hand to me. I stood.

"Let's walk outside," he said.

"Again you have come here unlooked for," I said when we went through the doorway.

"Again I have come to seek you," he said. "I owe you a debt of thanks."

"For what?"

"For taking me to the men of this place. The overthrow of Eglon began here, in Beth-Zur."

I shrugged. "It was little enough to do."

"But of such little the Most High sometimes makes much."

The dream. The Voice. The blessing...

His hand was on my arm. "What is it?"

I pulled in a deep breath. "A dream I had."

"When I came in you were asleep. The woman said you had been sleeping for an entire night and a day. She said you cried and called out strangely. I heard you myself, just before she woke you."

"A night and a day?"

He nodded.

I looked toward the west, toward the crown of the Hill of Zur. "I dreamed of the Most High."

He looked at me for a long moment, then nodded. "Yes. I see it in you."

There was a quiet space, then he said, "I am sorry about your mother."

"She was taken ill when I returned from Jericho."

"Yes, so the woman told me."

We walked a few paces.

He had stopped walking. He was staring into the distance.

"What's wrong?"

He looked at me. "Jabez, I... There is something I must tell you. You told me once in Jebus that you had no father. How much do you know of your mother's life... before?"

Something like fear prickled at the nape of my neck. I couldn't speak.

"Let me tell you a story," he said. He put his arm around my shoulder and we walked, round and round my house as the day faded into afternoon, round and round as the darkness settled onto the world, round and round as his voice opened a path into the past, into places I was not sure I wanted to go.

There was a man of Benjamin, he said, who was always getting into trouble. He was hotheaded and quick-tongued and often in the wrong place at the wrong time. For all that, Ehud said, he was a good friend, and a true one. He might wound with his words, but he was quick to repent, extravagant in his atonements.

He made enemies of the wrong people, though, and found it easier to leave the territory of Benjamin than to continually watch his back. He traveled south, into Judah. He traveled until he came to a small village in the hills, a place called Beth-Zur.

"You have maybe heard of the love that sometimes happens between a man and woman," Ehud said. "Sometimes when the eyes of two people meet, it is as if they have known each other already, as if they are meeting the other part of themselves. Father Jacob knew such a love for Rachel, it is said. The stories say he was so moved by his love for her that he lifted a heavy well stone so her flocks could drink. They say he wept aloud for the beauty of her."

Such a love, Ehud told me, fell out of the blue sky upon this Benjamite and a young woman of Beth-Zur. But the woman was betrothed to another. Her name was Libnah.

The Benjamite knew it was a sin to look upon a woman promised to another, Ehud said. He knew speaking to her was wrong. Each night before he slept he promised himself and the Most High he would leave the next day and never return. But each morning he went to the well and waited for her to come and draw water. Each morning she would see him waiting, see the love in his eyes.

He would see the way she looked at him, and he knew. They both knew. And they both knew it could never be.

On the day she went into the house of her husband, he left Beth-Zur. He felt as a man feels when he has lost an arm. He felt as if the joy had been drained out of him and replaced with brine. He vowed never to look at another woman. He vowed to seek death rather than embrace someone he could never love.

"For he had given her his heart, Jabez. He could never get it back."

The Benjamite traveled around Judah. In his travels, he crossed paths with an old friend from home, another Benjamite who had gone on to other places. The two men traveled together for a while. They had adventures. But something was gone from the first man, Ehud said. A light was extinguished inside him. He told his friend of the woman he had seen in Beth-Zur, the woman whose name meant "Brightness."

"He began to take bigger and bigger chances," Ehud said. "He would make thoughtless boasts, then take terrible risks to make them good. He fought more, drank more. He looked for trouble. And then, one day…you can guess the way of it."

We sat for a long time when he quit talking. The moon was rising, a fat, orange melon on the eastern horizon.

"So you think the Libnah in your story is the woman lying in this house on her deathbed?"

He shrugged. "I gave you a story. You have to decide what to do with it."

I looked at him. His eyes were sad, like one who looks down a long, narrow passage and knows he must travel its length, willing or not.

"Tomorrow I will go back to Gilgal," he said. "But maybe I will come again to Beth-Zur."

"Maybe I will come to Gilgal," I said. "Who knows?"

We went back into the house. My mother's eyes were open. Ahuzzah looked up at me from beside her mat.

"She has been calling for you."

"I was just outside," I said. "Why didn't you—"

"Not you," Ahuzzah said. She nodded toward Ehud. "Him."

Ehud kneeled beside my mother. He placed a hand alongside her cheek. "Are you Libnah?" he said in the tenderest voice I had ever heard him use.

Her eyes fluttered, but held. "The Benjamite," she said in a voice like the whisper of a moth's wing. "You... remind me of him."

"He died for love of you, rather than dishonor you," Ehud said. "That is a thing not every woman can say."

"No. Not every woman." I thought she tried to smile. Her lips moved.

Ehud beckoned me. "She wants to speak to you," he said.

I put my ear to her lips, straining with every fiber to catch the faint breath of her words.

"You were born in pain," she said, "but not in shame."

"Yes, Mother. I know. I understand."

"On the day you were born, they told me of the death of my beloved. I named you from the hurt of that. I cursed you with my pain. I am sorry."

"Do not speak, Mother. It is all right. It is—"

"Peace, my son. Peace…"

The last word sighed from her upon the ending of her breath. She was gone. I placed my fingertips on her eyelids and closed them. Behind me I heard quiet sobbing. It was Raboth. I held out my arms to him, and he rushed to me. We held each other. We wept. What else was there to do?

E P I L O G U E

Sometimes I think my whole life is what came after.

The days in Beth-Zur were very different after that—at least, for a long time they were. For many years we had peace. Raboth and I farmed our land and cared for our olive trees. In time, he came to be a better husbandman than I. We never lacked for either food or something left over to trade. Ahuzzah never became skilled in the ways of food, but our bellies were never empty. I think she even came to tolerate me, after her fashion.

I took for my wife Maacah, the daughter of Jachin, a man from Tekoa, just over the hills east of Beth-Zur. Thinking of it still makes me smile. I was in Tekoa to trade for a milking goat. It was a thirsty walk, up and down among the crags of the high country, and my first thought upon reaching Tekoa was to find the well. And there I saw Maacah, drawing water for her mother. I was caught like a fly in a web. I remember thinking that surely the Most High had sent me to Tekoa that day, just as he sent Father Jacob to the well of his kinsman. I did not have to move a stone for her, but I would have tried.

In those days, it was thought a good thing to marry a daughter to one who had been to the battle at the fords of the Jordan. I know it was a good thing for me; I had little enough for a bride price back then. But her father saw the love in my face and it made him glad, I think. Maacah bore me two sons and a daughter.

I do not say that Maacah and I have the kind of love that my mother felt for the Benjamite, but to us, the love we have seems good indeed. We have cared for each other through the good years and the lean ones. It still pleases me to look at her, even though her face is wrinkled and her hair is no more the thick, gleaming black of the day of our wedding. I think she still takes some pleasure in the touch of my hand on her cheek.

A few years passed and the man died who had farmed the land adjoining ours. His name was Zoheth; he had no heir. I helped bind his body for burial and some of my neighbors and I carried him to the caves. When the fathers cast the lot to see who would receive his goods, it fell to me. Raboth and I suddenly found ourselves with another field as well as a good she-donkey for plowing. On the day I learned of it, I went to the top of the Hill of Zur and bowed low before the Most High.

Raboth and I decided he should take Zoheth's ground to farm for himself. It lay along a creek bed that was dry except in the winter and early spring; it was flatter than the land we already had and much less stony. Raboth seeded it in barley and millet and in later years planted a vineyard on the better-drained parts. He figured out a way to store some of the winter runoff from the creek and use it for summer irrigation; men used to come from as far away as Hebron to discover how he had done it. There were a few dry years when our fields yielded as much as everyone else's put together. I felt as proud of Raboth as a father feels for a son, watching him explain his contrivance to those who journeyed to see it. And the extra bounty of our fields enabled us to help many who would have otherwise been hungry.

His sons still farm the land, though through the years our fields have grown far beyond that small beginning. They are good boys. They still ask my advice from time to time, but I think they only do it to humor me; their father can teach them more than I will ever know. I don't mind it though. One of my chief joys is to go out during the harvest and watch Raboth and his sons laboring side by side with my sons and their sons. Watching their strong arms rise and fall with the sickles, listening to their laughter as they work is as good to me as a feast of fat mutton and honeycomb. When the boys come to where I sit and embrace me, the moisture of their honest sweat is like an anointing with precious oil.

Once or twice I have walked out to the fields alone when the spring rains were falling. I have let the water run down my face, and I have lifted my eyes to the green hills beyond our fields, and I have breathed deeply the good, clean smell of rain falling on tilled ground. It pleases me to imagine I hear Ehud laughing with me, as he did in my dream long ago. I imagine I hear the echo of a song.

I see some of the younger men in the town burning incense at the Asherah pole and the roadside baals. That is not good. The Nameless One brooks no rivals, I tell them. They smile at me and thank me for my words. Sometimes they give me a pot of figs or raisins for my trouble. I do not need their favors. I wish they would listen to me. Some of them do, maybe. Enough of them that the old stories will stay alive, I hope.

About the time our third child was born, there started to be a little trouble, off and on, with the sea people. They were outgrowing the plains beside the Great Sea, and some of their nobles were starting to eye the valleys of the hill country as a good place to expand their borders. So far, they have not come this much to the east. I think there will have to be more fighting with them, but I do not think I will live long enough to see it. I pray for my children and their children; they may see some hard times. It may be that the Most High will raise up another strong man like Ehud to save his people. Maybe he will be a Benjamite too, who knows?

━━━━━━━

I am older than most of the people left in Beth-Zur. Most of the women who avoided my mother and me at the well have been sleeping in the caves for many years. All of the men who heard my brother's hateful words at the olive presses are long dead. Now I am one of the fathers. Younger men come to me to settle disputes or to ask for wisdom. Sometimes men come to me to ask what dowry they should send with their daughters.

Some of the older men still remember me as the friend of Ehud, the one who delivered us from the Moabites. I do not think it was mere chance that brought me to Jebus on that night so long ago, nor chance that the tall, left-handed soldier stayed the hands that would have slit my throat. Boys come to hear the stories of old days. Some of them still remember the story of Ehud. They ask about the knife, and I have to tell them with a laugh that I never knew what finally became of that blade. It is probably hanging in the house of somebody's grandfather who lives in Jericho. But I tell them about Ehud, about his long legs and his broad shoulders. And about the word that came to him from the Most High. When they let me, I try to skip over the killing parts. That is not the part I like to tell. Mothers bring their newborn children to me for a blessing; that is my favorite thing.

In spite of all the living I have done though, I still think about that sundown on the top of the Hill of Zur. My little stack of rocks is still there; I have kept it up, all these years. Sometimes I go there and think about my mother and her broken heart. Sometimes I go there when I am feeling the sadness of Jashub's memory, or when I want to think about the many joys Maacah and I have had during our years together. But more often, I go there to think about all the ways the Most High has been good to me. In a way, I guess, that is all the same thing.

I realize now that as much as I longed to know him, I did not truly know the One to whom I prayed that night. And even though my shoulders are stooped with age and my head is almost barren of hair, I think I still do not really know him. Maybe no man knows him, not the way a man can know his friends or his family anyway. He is beyond knowing.

But he knows me. And that has made the difference.

I am one of the old ones, one of the last remaining brave men of Gilgal. My friends in Beth-Zur look at me and see long years and long memories.

But when I look at myself, I still see the youth, barely more than a boy, who craved more than anything to know his place in the world. I see the boy who knew his mother's tears, but not her smile. I see the boy, surprised by the beauty of a sunset, who asked the great and terrible Beauty for something he could not even understand.

It is good, maybe, that we cannot understand some things. If we asked only for what we understood, I think our lives would be much poorer than they are. Sometimes we gain so much more than we are expecting.

It has been so with me.

This is a work of historical fiction based on Judges 3:12-15, 17:6, and 1 Chronicles 4:9-10. The Bible does not give us the complete story of Jabez's life, nor of the lives of other biblical figures that unfold in these pages. While artistic license has been taken where events, dialogue, and additional characters are concerned, every effort has been made to maintain scriptural and historical accuracy.

═══════════

*A free, downloadable reading group guide
to this novel is available at
www.waterbrookpress.com*